The Devil's Henchmen

MICHAEL C. DE LA PEÑA

Disclaimer: *The Devil's Henchmen* is a work of fiction. Similarities to any persons, living or dead, are only a coincidence.

Also by Michael C. de la Peña:

The Coyote Wars

The Last Coyote

Coyote Rising

To the brave police officers of the National Academy Session 274-Section 3, with whom I had the honor of sharing time.

Be safe out there!

It is by its promise of a sense of power that evil often attracts the weak.

—Eric Hoffer (1902–1983), American philosopher and author

ONE

Pain

Alicia Webster lay in a bed at New Haven Medical Center, and she was shrieking. Not the shrieks of childbirth. A primordial scream, which sent shivers down the spine of the two nurses who were tending to her. Her grip on the metal rim of the bed was viselike. She seemed on the verge of breaking the bed frame. Dr. Wilson was the lead physician, and he motioned for them to move aside. Max, her devoted husband, was ordered out of the room. He paced nervously outside, his mind racing. *It wasn't supposed to be like this*, he thought. He kept repeating that like a mantra, hoping to change the course of events. But he knew it was useless. His mind rewound its memory, to a better place.

Alicia Webster had always wanted a child. She knew at a very young age that motherhood was her goal. It seemed so old-fashioned growing up that she told almost nobody. Except for Max; he did know. She shared her desire to start a family. So it was no surprise to them when she became pregnant within two months of their wedding. Looking back on it, he smiled momentarily, thinking of how she gave him the news. One morning, she woke before he did, which was unusual. When he went into the bathroom, she had placed the fertility stick on the sink, next to his shaving cream. He couldn't miss it. He went back to bed, and they made love. This made him late for work, but it didn't matter. They had true happiness.

Now, as Max waited for news, that all seemed a quaint notion.

Ten minutes passed, and Dr. Wilson emerged from the room. As he approached Max, his face betrayed bad news. Max started shaking, as the doctor put a hand on his shoulder.

"I'm sorry, Mr. Webster; your child was stillborn."

Max wept, tears streaming down his face. He felt as though he might collapse. The doctor must have sensed it, because he escorted him by the elbow to a chair.

"And Alicia?" he finally stammered.

"We've sedated her. We will keep her overnight for observation. She's being moved now to a room."

"Was it a boy or a girl?" Max cried.

"It was a girl. I'm sorry."

Max shook his head in despair.

"I'll have someone take you to her room in a few minutes. Please wait here."

With that, the doctor slipped away. He had been a doctor long enough to be wary of emotional entanglements. He could not cry with every family. He had a job to do.

Milton Verdun, a young orderly at New Haven Medical Center, pushed Alicia's bed down the long passageway and into an elevator. He had only been working there for two months, and this was the second mother to have a stillborn child in that time. Once he and Alicia were alone in the elevator, Milton smiled slyly and put his hand on her head. As they glided up five floors, he caressed her hair.

Alicia was unconscious and unaware of Milton's presence. The elevator reached the fifth floor, and he pushed the bed out and into the hallway. He found room 505 and slid the bed into its allotted slot, next to the monitoring equipment. He knew a nurse would be in shortly to attach the monitors to Alicia. But he knew he had a few moments alone with her.

He caressed her hand and leaned into her ear.

"Your pain is only just beginning, my sweet."

His voice was soft, like an evil hiss. Just then, he heard footsteps, and he stepped away from the bed.

TWO

Quantico NAC 93-03

It was the first day of class, a fact that it was obvious to an astute observer. The forty-two students were seated alphabetically and shifted anxiously in their seats. A package of materials lay before each student. Among the items included in the packet were a curriculum, a legal handbook, and an FBI Code of Conduct manual. Two people stood before the class. Special Agent (SA) Christopher Nuggle was not an instructor. He was an evaluator. He stood next to Legal Instructor Vance Collins, who was reviewing his notes. Collins was strictly concerned with the legal aspects of his instruction. Nuggle, on the other hand, was busy observing the entire class. His job, at least in his mind, was to mold this group of civilians into special agents of the FBI.

As Nuggle watched the class, he noticed an anomaly in the back of the group. One of the students was sitting serenely, motionless. While the other students read portions of their introductory materials, this student left them untouched on the desk in front of him. At one point, the student leaned back, lacing his hands behind his head.

A vein in Nuggle's neck began throbbing. His face was getting red. He read the nameplate in front of the student. "Sullivan," it read. He turned to a small table next to him, which contained the students' biographies. He ran his index finger down the directory until he found the name.

"Carlos Sullivan," he whispered to himself.

"Twenty-six years old, from Boston," Nuggle said softly. Even Collins, standing next to him, couldn't hear what he said. *I won't forget that name*, he thought.

He put the thought aside to begin his introduction.

"Ladies and Gentlemen," Nuggle said, clapping his hands once, "welcome to Quantico."

The group snapped to attention, putting their packets down.

"You are New Agent Class (NAC) 93-03," he began, "the third class of 1993, and much is expected of you."

As Nuggle continued to lay out the agenda for the next sixteen weeks of instruction, most of the students were taking notes. Sullivan was not. He didn't need to. He was listening intently. There was no need for note-taking.

*****

Two weeks later, Sullivan and his roommate, Jonathan Turley, had become fast friends. This was especially fortunate for Sullivan, because he didn't make friends easily. Within two days of meeting, Turley had stopped calling his roommate "Carlos" and simply used the moniker "Sully."

Turley saw something in Sullivan that made him comfortable. He had essentially decided to hitch his wagon to the cocky Bostonian, despite the rumors that he had already pissed off the lead evaluator for NAC 93-13. Sullivan, for his part, had convinced Turley that together they would get the best marks for the first legal exam, which was the next morning. Turley was nervous despite his confidence in Sullivan, who had the unorthodox idea of playing pool as part of their study session.

So it was that Sullivan and Turley were playing pool in the lobby of the FBI Academy's Washington dorm at 10:00 p.m., while their counterparts were locked in their rooms, cramming. Sullivan had already read the legal handbook twice, once more that he really needed to. His method was to quiz Turley every time one of them took a shot. As Turley lined up his cue stick, Sullivan leaned over.

"When is Miranda applicable?" he asked.

"When you have custodial interrogation. *Both* custody and interrogation must be in play," Turley answered.

Then he hit the cue ball against number 6, banking it into the pocket.

"Excellent," Sullivan replied.

"Sully, you realize if we score under an eighty percent, we get put on probation, right?"

"Eighty? You're crazy. I'll eat that cue stick if we get anything under a ninety percent." Sully laughed.

"I hope you're right, my friend," Turley said hopefully.

"Let's move on to Fourth Amendment exceptions."

Turley nodded in agreement.

They continued their ritual, with Turley also asking questions.

They did this until midnight. During that time, several of their classmates had passed by, having gone downstairs to get coffee. To them, it seemed as though team Sully and Turley were thoroughly enjoying themselves, oblivious to the test in the morning. They shook their heads. Sullivan noticed, but it didn't bother him. He smiled.

*****

The next afternoon Nuggle was in his office reviewing some reports, when the telephone rang loudly on his desk. He could see from the caller ID that it was Collins. He picked up right away.

"What's up, Vance?"

"You wanted to be the first to know."

"Know what?" Nuggle asked, puzzled.

"The Sullivan kid, remember?"

"Oh right."

"Well, he scored a perfect one hundred." Collins chuckled.

"Damn," Nuggle said, disappointed.

"His friend Turley scored a ninety-eight. And I heard they were up all night playing pool."

"Maybe they cheated."

“Nope, I was watching them. They are the real deal, buddy.”

“He’ll slip up. The cocky ones always do. Thanks for the heads-up.”

Nuggle softly cradled the receiver and grimaced.

THREE

Mail

Following her miscarriage, Alicia Webster had taken time off from work. Max had also taken a week off, but now he needed to get back to his job as a regional manager for an insurance company in Hartford. He had no choice. His industry was particularly cutthroat. There was always someone waiting in the wings to take his job should he falter. He had hated the idea of leaving Alicia alone. She had cried for three straight days. When she awoke every morning, her eyes were puffy and red. He wasn't sure how long the grieving process would take. It had hit Alicia hard.

From her living room, Alicia had a clear view of the street. She checked her watch and realized it was almost 3:00 p.m. Max had called her three times already. She knew that she needed to just shake it off, but she couldn't get the sight of her dead baby staring at her out of her mind.

In time, she thought. Just then, she saw the mail truck briefly stop in front of her residence. She left her cup of tea on the coffee table to see what the mailman had dropped off.

There were two letters. One was her utility bill addressed to Max. The other was addressed to her. Her name and address were handwritten in bold letters. It had no return address, but it seemed a bit bulky on one end.

Alicia opened it as she entered her house. She unfolded the letter the envelope contained, and something slipped out of it and fell on the floor. She looked down and felt sick at the sight of a baby's little finger. The blood started to drain from her head, and the room started to spin.

The letter fell out of her hand as she fell unconscious onto the carpeted floor.

******

Detective John Saucier had been with the Wallingford Police Department for over fifteen years. In all that time, he had never received a complaint like the one described by his lieutenant. He rang the Webster doorbell not knowing what to expect. Max had been waiting and opened the door instantly.

"I'm Detective Saucier. May I come in?"

Max held open the door.

"Of course." He waved Saucier in.

Saucier looked about and noticed they were alone.

"Your wife?"

"She's in bed resting. She's been through a lot."

"Of course," Saucier said, relieved that he wouldn't be talking to the victim.

"Have a seat," Max said. "I'll get the letter."

"Actually, just take me to the letter," Saucier said as he retrieved a pair of gloves from his jacket.

"Oh right." He hesitated. "It's in the kitchen."

On the counter was the letter and envelope. Next to it was an oversize napkin. Max had wrapped the finger with the napkin.

Saucier inspected the letter with a gloved hand. It was handwritten in block-lettering style. He read the letter silently.

ALICIA, YOUR WOMB BELONGS TO SATAN. YOU BELONG TO HIM ALONE. YOUR LITTLE GIRL IS WITH HIM NOW.

Max watched as Saucier finished reading the letter.

"Do you understand how this affected my wife?" he pleaded.

"I can imagine, Mr. Webster."

He took a small evidence bag and placed the napkin and its contents in it, sealing it.

"When was her miscarriage?" Saucier asked, retrieving a notebook.

"One week ago, at New Haven Medical Center."

"Is that our little girl's finger?"

Saucier hesitated. "I have to ask, about the baby…the arrangements?"

“Oh yes, I’m afraid we had the child cremated. We couldn’t bear the strain of burying her.”

“I see,” Saucier said dejectedly, knowing this would preclude an inspection of the corpse.

“I’m going to look into it, Mr. Webster. Do you have any idea who might have a beef with you or your wife?”

“Not at all, Detective. We live a boring life. We don’t have enemies.” He shook his head.

“All right, I’ll keep you posted.”

“Thank you.”

“I’m also going to loop in the FBI,” he said flatly.

“The FBI?”

“Yes, the sender used the U.S. Postal Service. That makes this a federal crime.”

As Saucier walked down the front steps of the Webster home, he wondered how sick a person had to be to send such a letter. He had already deduced that the sender must have a connection to the hospital. Before going there, he would stop in at the FBI. He had worked with a senior agent there on a bank robbery once before. Perhaps they could help.

FOUR

Theft and Friendship

Melissa Dobson had worked at the FBI Academy's library for almost eight years. She was always seen with a smile, large red glasses, and bright-red nail polish. This only accentuated her red hair, which she kept in a tight bun. She had two nicknames. Most people called her "Red" for obvious reasons. Others called her Hoover's secretary. She sat in the shadow of an enormous framed photo of J. Edgar Hoover leaning across his desk.

Whenever Sullivan stopped at the library, she always greeted him with a wave and a smile. This Saturday was no different, although it was unusual for her to be working on the weekend. He had grown accustomed to her sunny disposition in the month he had been at the academy. So it was with upsetting when he now noticed her crying into a tissue. Her face was red as she sobbed quietly.

"What's wrong, Red?" Sullivan said, kneeling next to her.

"I'm sorry, I shouldn't be crying." She waved the tissue in the air.

"Tell me what happened."

"Somebody stole my Kate Spade bag. It was an anniversary present."

"Oh." Sullivan hesitated. "What's a Kate Spade bag?"

Dobson stopped sobbing for a moment, as she chuckled.

"You are funny."

"Sorry, I just don't know what that is."

"It's just a *very* expensive purse. I just went to the bathroom, and now it's gone. Who would think it's not safe in here?" She shook her head.

"That is crazy."

"The worst part is my keys were inside the bag. I only have one car key. And my license and credit cards were in the bag." She started crying again.

Sullivan put a hand on her back to comfort her.

"I'll make sure you get a ride home tonight. In the meantime, I'll get the contents of your bag back."

Dobson's eyes widened.

"You will? How?" she asked, flustered.

"Don't worry; I'll take care of it, Red," he said calmly.

"Well, that would be some trick."

"I'm afraid the bag is gone. That's the bad news. The coworker who stole it, she was eyeing that for some time. That's all she wanted."

"I just can't believe it. Nothing is sacred." Her voice trailed off as she shook her head.

Sullivan stood up to leave.

"You can say that again."

*****

Carlos Sullivan without Jimmy Conrad was like Saturn without its rings. They were meant to coexist, and it seemed that they were always in each other's orbit. They had grown up together in Medford, Massachusetts, a blue-collar town just north of Boston. In truth, it had been Conrad who had the first impulse to join the FBI. Sullivan had never really given it any real thought. It was Conrad, whose father was a Medford patrolman, who wanted to join law enforcement. His enthusiasm had won over Sullivan. He was the reason Sullivan was at the FBI Academy. As luck would have it, Sullivan received his acceptance letter first. Conrad's letter came two weeks later.

Sullivan stood, arms crossed, leaning against a light pole in the academy's main parking lot as a blue Ford with Massachusetts plates pulled into a spot. Conrad was grinning as he turned off the ignition. *Of course*, he thought. Sullivan had to be the first to greet him. What he didn't realize was that Sullivan had been waiting for over an hour.

Conrad pulled his massive frame out of the Chevy as Sullivan approached. Sullivan hadn't seen his friend in three weeks. He was not typically emotional. So it was with some surprise when he gave Conrad a huge bear hug.

"You missed me, I see." Conrad smiled.

"Just a bit."

"Well, good. You can help me with my bags."

"Sure, rookie."

"Ha! Two weeks ahead of me and I'm the rookie, huh?"

"That's right, rookie. Let's go."

"How did you know when I'd be getting here?" Conrad queried him.

"Are you kidding? I could set my watch to you. I called Mom. She told me when you left Boston."

"Ah." He nodded.

As they walked into the academy's atrium, Sullivan looked over at his friend.

"Do you know what a Kate Spade bag is?"

"Who's Kate Spade?" Conrad made a face.

"No, the bag," Sullivan clarified.

"Why would I know about her bag?"

"Never mind." Sullivan shrugged.

*****

After escorting his friend to his room at the Jefferson dorm, Sullivan made a beeline to the computer room. In 1993, work computers were a new phenomenon in the FBI, but Sullivan understood the basics. He found a station with a working printer. Once logged in, he found the template for an official FBI memorandum. He started writing.

Earlier today, Mrs. Dobson's purse went missing. He left out a description. He knew that the thief knew exactly what she took. He kept typing. *Unfortunately, Mrs. Dobson's keys and identification were in the purse. Whoever borrowed the purse undoubtedly didn't mean to hurt Red by taking these items. Please return them as soon as possible*. He left the memo unsigned.

Sullivan deliberately left out any accusatory language. He was gambling on the thief's remorse. He printed fifty copies and spent the next hour putting the memorandum on as many doors at the academy he could find.

FIVE

Solution and Conflict

NAC 93-03 started Monday morning by running the "yellow brick road," a famous Marine Corps, 6.2 mile wooded running trail, which includes a series of obstacles. The FBI has special permission from the Marine Corps to run the course. Sullivan and Turley ran side by side. They had become friendly competitors. Sullivan always wanted to finish first. Turley, however, was faster. It was only June, but already the sun was strong and the heat thick.

In the lead was Fitness Instructor John Rogers, a legend at the FBI Academy. In his fifties, he could still outrun and outlast any of the students. He was also well known for his speeches. Some of the students used to joke that he would talk them into shape. Before each run, he would often tell the trainees he would work them so hard, they would sleep like babies. Then he invariably added, "You'll wake up every ten minutes and cry."

After completing the run, Rogers called the class together in a circle. He always had a speech ready. This one was about maintaining a proper diet.

"When you go to the cafeteria," he started, "do they charge you anything?"

The class didn't respond.

"I don't hear you?" He cupped his ear.

“No,” the class finally answered in unison.

“That’s right.” He pointed his finger at them, like a prosecutor. “But there is a price to be paid,” he added.

The group laughed.

“All right, guys, go shower. You’ll be late for legal.”

As they walked to the locker room, Sullivan patted Turley on the back.

“That guy cracks me up.”

*****

When Melissa Dobson arrived for work Monday morning, she couldn’t believe her eyes. Leaning against the library door was her license and credit cards wrapped in a rubber band. Next to that were her house and car keys.

“Well, I’ll be,” she whispered to herself. “The kid was right.”

*****

Sullivan was running late for class. In his haste, after showering, he had failed to tuck in his shirt. All FBI trainees are required to wear a uniform, consisting of brown khakis and a blue, short-sleeved polo shirt. The shirt must be tucked in. A brown belt is also required. As Sullivan walked down a hallway outside of the gym, Nuggle saw him and called him over. Turley was with Sullivan.

"Trainee Sullivan, come here please."

When Turley also approached, he waved him off.

"Not you, Turley; you are dismissed."

"Yes, sir," Sullivan answered.

"Trainee Sullivan, you are out of uniform." Nuggle pointed at his untucked shirt.

"Sorry, sir," Sullivan said, tucking his shirt in properly.

"That will be a suitability."

"Sir?"

"A suitability. Didn't you read the Code of Conduct manual, trainee?" Nuggle said with unconcealed contempt.

"What am I to do about it, sir? I'm sorry."

"There's nothing you can do. I'll be filing a formal suitability complaint. If you get two in one week, then you will be put up before the board."

Nuggle then turned and walked away.

Sullivan scratched his head. *That's not good*, he thought. That evening, Sullivan decided to reread the manual.

SIX

Despair

Paula White was an office administrator for the *New Haven Free Press*. Although she had a relatively low-level position, she had one of the best views of the city from her window. She looked outside as a late spring wind kicked up some leaves, causing them to flutter down the street. She was reviewing some files when, without warning, she started feeling a sharp pain in her belly. She was only seven months pregnant, so she knew something was definitely wrong. The pain was so abrupt and searing that she let out a yelp. This was followed by a gushing stream of vomit. One of her coworkers rushed to her side. In less than ten minutes, she was in an ambulance racing to the New Haven Medical Center.

By the time the ambulance arrived, Dr. Wilson and two nurses were already waiting. The ambulance crew wheeled her into the hospital and into an emergency room. By the time Dr. Wilson emerged from the room thirty minutes later, his patient's husband was sitting in the waiting area.

Head nurse Flaherty whispered in Dr. Wilson's ear as he stood outside the ER, flipping some charts.

He shook his head as he approached Brian White. The husband wasn't crying yet. Wilson knew that would come later. First, a state of confusion washed over the survivors. They were often emotionless as they received the news. Devastation would envelop them later. He saw the signs in Mr. White as he got closer.

As he processed the news, Brian White shook his head. He started to stammer.

"How can this be?" He paused. "She was the picture of health."

"I'm afraid sometimes these things happen."

White sat down, both hands cradling his head.

Dr. Wilson stood awkwardly. He hated this part of his job the most. He also had other patients. He looked about for a way out. Finally, he leaned down.

"I'm sorry for your loss, Mr. White. Somebody will be with you in a few minutes."

White reached out and grabbed his arm. "Can I see my wife?"

"She's sedated; someone will escort you to her room once it's ready."

Wilson then made a hasty retreat to his office.

Several minutes later, Milton Verdun pushed Mrs. White's bed down the hallway and into the hospital elevator. He pressed button number five. Once alone with her, he began caressing her hair.

"You are so beautiful," he said softly. "I'm sorry, but your child was the devil's spawn."

Verdun then moved from the head of the bed to its side. He began rubbing her belly.

"Oh yes, your womb carried the devil himself."

In that moment, the elevator stopped, and the door opened on the fifth floor. Verdun moved back to the end of the bed and pushed it out of the elevator. He slid the bed into room 505, the same room previously used by Alicia Webster. He chuckled at the thought.

SEVEN

Judgment

One week after the incident with Melissa Dobson, Sullivan was resting in his dorm bed. Classes were over for the day, and he was just plain tired. There would be no pool playing or even studying. Turley went out to dinner with a couple of other classmates. He knew this was his opportunity to just relax in his room by himself. Two minutes into his relaxation strategy, he heard a rap on the door.

Reluctantly, he got up and opened the door.

To his surprise, it was Bianca Tierney, one of his classmates. Alphabetically, she was seated two down from him in class. They had never spoken.

"What's up?"

"Chris Nuggle sent me. He said you are to report to his office at eight a.m. sharp tomorrow."

"I see."

She turned to leave.

"Do you know what this is about?"

"No idea, Sullivan; sorry."

As she walked down the hall, he had the feeling she was lying. She knew something.

Later that evening, Turley shook his head as Sullivan recounted the cryptic message he had received.

"Why would numb nuts Nuggle want to see you?"

"That's cute."

"That's what everyone's been calling him." Turley chuckled.

"I have no idea. But it can't be good."

As they talked, they heard another knock on the door. This time, the visitor knocked and entered. It was Conrad.

"What's going on?" he started. "Everyone's saying you're jammed up."

"So the rumor mill is swirling," Sullivan said.

"Yeah, everyone in my class already heard about your appointment tomorrow. Word is that numb nuts Nuggle has it in for you."

"So it would seem."

"What did you do?" Conrad asked, puzzled.

Sullivan sat on the end of his bed, arms crossed.

"I guess we'll find out tomorrow."

******

When Sullivan entered Nuggle's office in the morning as instructed, he knew immediately what the matter involved. Lying squarely in front of Nuggle was the Dobson memo he had created in the computer lab. Sullivan started calculating what infraction they would be charging him with. Sullivan pointed at one of the chairs in front of Nuggle's desk.

"Shall I sit, Mr. Nuggle?"

"No, you shall not, Trainee Sullivan," he answered icily.

Sullivan shrugged slightly. This further infuriated Nuggle.

"Trainee Sullivan"—Nuggle reached for the memo—"did you write this memorandum?"

"I did, sir."

"Did you receive official permission to create this document?"

"No, sir."

"Very well then. This incident has cost you two suitabilities."

"Two?" Sullivan was incredulous.

"Yes, one is for unauthorized production of an official FBI communication. The other for improper dissemination of the said document."

"That seems a bit extreme," Sullivan countered.

"Do you know what this means, Trainee Sullivan?" Nuggle smirked.

Sullivan knew all too well. He had reread the manual after his first suitability.

"Yes, sir. Two suitabilities in one week means I will be brought before the NARB—the new agents review board."

"That is correct. You are suspended from attending classes today. Your review board will meet tomorrow morning. You are dismissed."

Sullivan arched an eye as Nuggle dismissed him with a wave of his right hand.

As Sullivan walked down the hallway toward his dormitory building, he knew that the NARB was an effective death sentence. Almost every case resulted in dismissal from the academy. He took in his surroundings, assuming that he would most likely be gone in twenty-four hours.

*****

That evening, Sullivan held counsel in the cafeteria with Conrad and Turley. They found an isolated table at the far end of the cafeteria. They had noticed the stares Sullivan was getting from the other students. Everyone was talking about the incident. Sullivan swirled the ice in his cup of soda as his friends quizzed him.

"So you wrote that memo?" Turley smiled.

"Sure did."

"How did Nuggle find out?" Conrad inquired.

"Red must have told someone. She didn't mean to hurt me obviously."

"I guess we'll file this under 'No good deed goes unpunished.'" Turley shook his head.

"Well, this was an interesting experience while it lasted."

"Since when do you give up so easily?" Conrad snapped.

"Look, I'll defend myself, but at the end of the day, we all know what the end result will be. I'm guilty. I didn't get permission to write the damn memo."

They all leaned back in their chairs. Conrad sat pensively, scratching his chin. He was the last to speak.

"Sully, you taught me that there are always options."

******

That evening, once all were asleep, Sullivan struggled to doze off. He lay in bed, eyes wide open, staring at the ceiling. Turley snored lightly. Sullivan envied his friend's peaceful slumber. He checked the clock, which read 2:12 a.m. Quietly, Sullivan slipped out of bed and put on his sneakers. He walked down the hall and took the stairs to the first floor, avoiding the noisy, clunky elevator.

Once outside, he headed for Hogan's Alley. The FBI created Hogan's Alley in 1987 as a training tool. It is a fake town, complete with a bank, pharmacy, motel, movie theater, and apartment buildings—all designed for recreating crime scenarios. The bank has been dubbed the "most robbed bank in the world." During the day, paid actors commit different crimes, while the agent trainees conduct investigations, to include surveillances and arrests. It is not uncommon for observers and visitors to hear agents shouting at the actors during the scenarios. Hogan's Alley is usually a beehive of activity. Now, in the dead of night, only crickets could be heard.

In 1993, the area around Quantico was relatively undeveloped. As a result, the night sky was alive with light. Sullivan made his way to the one-story motel, the Dogwood Inn. He knew from one of his training sessions that the back door did not lock. He slipped inside and found a staircase, which led to a trapdoor and then the roof. He thought it humorous that he was now actually committing an offense that could get him in trouble. He was sure Nuggle would love to see him climbing up to the roof. Once on top of the motel, Sullivan lay down on the brown, slanted roof. In the clear, cloudless night sky, Sullivan was in a real-life planetarium. Thousands of blinking lights illuminated the night. As he watched the cosmos in wonderment, he pondered the nature of his existence. In such a limitless universe, what role could he have to play?

He left Hogan's Alley that night with the belief that he was destined to do some good in the world. Whether that would be within the FBI was the only thing left to be decided.

EIGHT

Recurrence

After losing her child, Paula White went into a period depression. Three days after being released from the hospital, she visited her primary-care physician, Dr. Wayne Shoptrain. He had twenty years of experience and had a flair for comforting his patients. She sat on the end of the small bed in his observation room, her head down, shoulders slumped.

"Doctor, I wake up in the morning, and I don't want to get out of bed." A tear formed at the corner of her eye.

The doctor stood next to her, his stethoscope draped over his shoulder.

"That is normal, Paula. This will take a while to process. In the meantime, I will prescribe you an antidepressant medication."

"How could this happen, Doctor? My first pregnancy went without a hitch."

"Unfortunately, stillbirths occur in a small percentage of cases, even after having a child previously," he counseled.

"It just seems so unreal." She was now sobbing.

He patted her on the back.

"As long as you're here, I'll take some blood work."

The doctor stepped out and called his assistant to draw her blood.

******

When Paula White drove home that afternoon, she noticed that the mailman had forgotten to close the lid on her mailbox. She walked over to the box robotically. There was nothing ever really good in the mail. It was usually just a bill or a flyer. As she walked up her driveway, she sifted through several letters, one of which caught her attention. It was addressed to her. Unlike the others, it was handwritten in bold letters. There was no return address. It seemed to be a bit bulky on one end. She opened it carefully, peering inside.

When she saw the baby's tiny bloody finger, she fell to the ground, hitting her head. She lay unconscious on the pavement, bleeding.

******

By the time Detective Saucier arrived at New Haven Medical Center, Paula White was sedated, a bandage on her head and an IV drip inserted in her left arm. Brian White sat next to her bed, with his two-year-old son, Nicholas, on his lap, sleeping. The detective put his hand up, signaling White to stay seated. He pulled up a chair.

"Can we talk?" he asked.

White nodded in agreement.

“I have the letter and the finger. I have to tell you this was not personal. Another woman received the same type of package two weeks earlier.”

“Oh no.” White’s eyes widened.

“Yes, I’m afraid so. Coincidentally, that family also resides in Wallingford.”

“Who could write such horrible things…” His voice trailed off.

“A sick person, obviously.”

“So this other family got the same letter from this sicko?”

“A similar letter, yes. Do you know the Webster family, on Eagle Drive?” Saucier tried making a connection.

White hesitated, thinking. “No, I’ve never heard of them.”

Dejected, Saucier pocketed his notepad. As he did so, a young orderly came into the room. The name on his shirt read “Verdun.” Saucier looked over at him but gave him no special attention. He was clearing out the small trash can and replacing the plastic liner. They could not tell he was listening intently.

“What can I do?”

“Nothing really. I have an appointment with the FBI later today. They will hopefully be helping me find out who did this.”

Verdun's ears twitched when he heard the words "FBI." He slowed to a crawl. He didn't want to leave the room.

"I have to ask you, what arrangements did you make with your child?" He winced uncomfortably.

"We had his body sent to McCormick's Funeral Home. We want a proper burial."

"So he wasn't cremated?" Saucier perked up.

"No. We're traditional."

Saucier stood up. "With your permission, I want to inspect his body."

"Of course," White said.

In his excitement to leave, Saucier failed to notice Verdun watching him closely. Once he was gone, he turned to White.

"Would you care for some water, Mr. White?" he asked helpfully.

******

Having called ahead from a payphone, the director and owner of McCormick's Funeral Home, Michael McCormick, was waiting at the door when Saucier arrived. He was the third-generation McCormick to run the home. Gerald McCormick, his son, stood behind him. He was in training at the business. Both were dressed in dark suits, as was their custom.

Saucier pulled his police cruiser into a visitors' spot and climbed the eight steps to the front door, which opened as he landed on the platform.

"Detective Saucier, I presume." McCormick Senior extended a hand.

"Correct," he answered as McCormick ushered him inside the funeral home.

"Take me to the body, please." Saucier was curt. He was always curt when he had a hot lead.

They walked down a set of stairs into the basement, where fresh corpses were kept refrigerated. Baby White was kept in a plastic bin. McCormick removed the cover for the detective. His son, Gerald, observed from behind.

Saucier winced at the sight of the discolored fetus. *So tiny*, he thought. Immediately, Saucier inspected his hands.

"Well, that is a surprise," he said aloud.

"What were you looking for, Detective?"

"I *was* looking for a missing finger."

"As you can see, the baby is intact."

"Yes, I see that, Mr. McCormick. The plot has just thickened."

Standing behind his father and the detective, neither could see the smirk on Gerald's face.

NINE

Trial

On the morning of Sullivan's hearing, he made a point of doing two things before appearing before the board. The first was to have a large breakfast. He was eating for free, so he might as well enjoy his last meal. Secondly, he made a point of saying good-bye to Conrad and Turley. The former, he would certainly see again, as they were lifelong friends. Turley, however, might be assigned to a far-flung corner of the country, never to be seen again. And he had been kind to Sullivan.

Now Sullivan sat in a simple wooden chair in the middle of the room. In front of him were five people seated before a large conference table. Those were his judges, essentially. Sullivan was at peace with the situation, and he was relaxed, in large part because of his nighttime sky gazing. Having read the student manual twice, he knew that a simple majority was required for expulsion. He was ready for that judgment, as this was typically the only punishment. Suspension as a punishment served no purpose. If you were suspended and missed critical training, how could you later graduate with your class? As he looked to the board members, he could see he had already lost one vote. Nuggle sat in the fifth slot, a bemused grimace on his face. In the center, he recognized Brian Gavigan, the New Agents' Training Unit chief. He shuffled some papers as the other members took their seats. Sullivan recognized none of the others.

Sullivan noticed an additional female staff member sitting separately to the side, behind a desk. He recognized her as a secretary at the New Agents' Training Unit. He vaguely recalled her name was Carol. Sullivan assumed she served in some administrative capacity, perhaps as a notetaker.

Gavigan opened the proceedings.

"Trainee, are you aware of the purpose of this hearing?"

"I am."

"Do you have any questions before we formally introduce ourselves for the record?"

"So there will be a record?" Sullivan inquired, tilting his head slightly.

Gavigan paused, taken aback by Sullivan's aggressiveness. In his experience, most trainees in this situation groveled before him. *Perhaps the stories about him were true*, he thought for a moment. He then looked over at Carol.

"Yes, there will be a record."

"Very well, then I do have a question."

"What is your question, trainee?" Gavigan asked impatiently.

"I see that Mr. Nuggle is present. Will he be one of the voting members on this matter?"

"Yes, he will be."

"Is that not a conflict?" Sullivan snapped.

“This board has existed long before your attendance here at the academy, trainee. Our procedures are time-tested.”

“Very well. I simply wanted it recorded that Mr. Nuggle is the person who has written me up. As such, it seems unlikely he could vote impartially as a result,” Sullivan stated, looking over at Carol, who involuntarily arched an eye.

“Are you impugning Mr. Nuggle’s character?” Gavigan raised his voice. Nuggle simultaneously crossed his arms.

“No. Just his impartiality.”

Gavigan leaned back in his seat. He looked to his left and right, as if seeking the approval from his board members. Nuggle shook his head in disapproval.

“Your objection is overruled. We will proceed.”

Sullivan shrugged in his dismissive manner. Nuggle smiled slyly. He was quite sure he was close to finishing off his target.

Gavigan then proceeded to introduce the rest of his board members, for the record. They all worked for Gavigan. He was clearly the man in charge. Once Gavigan finished with the formalities, he turned back to Sullivan, who sat quietly, unfazed.

“The matter before the board involves the unauthorized production and dissemination of an FBI memorandum.”

Sullivan nodded and raised his hand.

“Yes, trainee,” Gavigan said, frustrated.

"I can save us all some time. I admit my guilt. I wrote the memo. I disseminated the memo. Please proceed to the judgment phase," he said flatly.

Gavigan's eyes widened. He did not appreciate the impudent trainee dictating terms at his hearing. If he had a gavel, he would have slammed it on the table. Just as he was about to berate Sullivan, a knock was heard on the door. Gavigan looked at Carol, who then walked over to the door. The hearing was temporarily interrupted as Carol whispered something to whoever was on the other side of the door. After a minute, she closed the door and walked over to Gavigan. She leaned over and whispered something in his ear.

Sullivan watched as Gavigan's eyes appeared to bulge. A vein started throbbing in his neck, and his face reddened. Once Carol was seated again, Gavigan composed himself.

"We will take a recess to consider your admission of guilt, trainee. Please wait outside while we deliberate."

Sullivan rose and walked to the door. *That's interesting*, he thought.

When he entered the waiting area, he could see what had happened. Conrad was sitting in the room. Next to him, clearly agitated, was Melissa Dobson, her arms crossed and staring straight ahead. Conrad winked at Sullivan, who decided to sit at the far end of the room. He didn't want to interfere.

After five minutes, Carol appeared at the door and waved for Sullivan to return. As he walked back into the hearing room, he smiled at Conrad.

"Please take a seat, Trainee Sullivan," Gavigan ordered. He immediately noticed for the first time that Gavigan used his name.

Sullivan said nothing, waiting. Gavigan shifted in his seat and then looked at his board members. Nuggle looked much less enthusiastic than he did previously. The smirk had been removed from his face. Gavigan was ready to render the verdict.

"We have reviewed this situation. There are mitigating circumstances. In addition, your candor speaks to your character. A witness has come forward to vouch for you—a valued member of the team here at the academy. In light of your infraction, however, a formal reprimand will be placed in your file. You are dismissed."

Sullivan sat for a moment, unblinking. He wondered. *That's it?* When he realized the session was over, he stood up.

"Thank you," he said simply.

He walked out of the hearing room and back to his room.

******

That evening, Sullivan met with Conrad and Turley in the parking lot, away from prying eyes. They greeted each other with high fives.

"Okay, Jimmy, what happened?" Sullivan started.

Conrad smirked.

"After our discussion, I decided to have a chat with Red. She's quite fond of you, by the way."

"Yeah, but how—"

"Well," Conrad interrupted, "it turns out that she and Gavigan had been an item a couple of years back."

"All right, but—"

Conrad put a hand up.

"You're going to love this," Turley chimed in.

"It seems that *Mrs.* Gavigan would not be happy to hear about this relationship."

"Ah, I see." Sullivan's eyes widened.

"When I told her about your predicament, she was very eager to help."

"Red's so nice, he never thought she'd stand up to him." Sullivan shook his head.

"He was so terrified when he heard she was outside the hearing room," Conrad added.

"I could see it on his face."

They all chuckled in unison.

Conrad patted his friend on the back. "You dodged a bullet, buddy."

TEN

C-3

Tim Dalton was a twenty-three-year veteran of the FBI. Having started his career under J. Edgar Hoover, he was old school. He always wore a crisply pressed white shirt with a dark suit. He never smoked, seldom drank, and rarely cussed. Dalton did adjust somewhat to the times, when he stopped wearing the standard fedora all G-men used to wear. The days of fancy hats were over.

Dalton was not remotely ambitious. He had taken over as the supervisor of New Haven's violent-crimes squad, known as C-3, only at the request of his friend and mentor, the former special agent in charge. Dalton was known as the "bear" because of his intimidating size. It was thus with some irony that from his office in New Haven he had a view of a stuffed grizzly bear, which was on display at the corner bank. He always wondered what significance the bear had. He had thought of going into the bank and asking, but he never got around to it.

Dalton was glancing out his window as he listened to the supervisor who had just called him out of the blue. After hanging up the phone, he was not pleased. After a moment, he called his most senior agent, and trusted right hand, Ralph Boreman, into his office.

"What's up, boss?" Boreman asked, taking a seat.

"I just got a call from a supervisor at the academy. His name is Chris Nuggle. Have you heard of him?"

“Nope. Never.”

“Well, remember I told you we’re getting a new agent in a couple of weeks?”

“Right, Carlos Sullivan. It’s on the roster.”

“Well, this Nuggle is not a fan. Says this Sullivan is quite a character. He said some pretty bad things about this guy.”

“Great.” Boreman sighed. “That’s all we need.”

“I was thinking. What are we doing about that satanic-letters case?”

“Detective Saucier has been asking for a meeting. I’ve put him off for two weeks.”

“We can’t ignore him forever. I don’t want to damage our relations with the Wallingford Police,” Dalton said, leaning back in his chair.

The FBI had a reputation of not cooperating with local law enforcement. This was an image the bureau was trying to correct. This was on Dalton’s mind, as HQ had mandated greater cooperation with local police.

“I’m thinking of assigning that matter to Sullivan when he gets here.”

“Makes sense. It is a nothing case. What could he screw up?”

“A nothing case, Ralph?” Dalton inquired. “Weren’t these women sent body parts?”

"Yes, but the fetuses were already dead. These women had miscarriages. There have only been two cases. It's more a case of hurt feelings. I think putting the new kid on this is a good idea."

"Make it happen." Dalton nodded in agreement.

"Sounds good."

"And if he is an asshole," Dalton added, "*and* he screws it up, we can get rid of him while he's still on probation."

ELEVEN

Graduation

After the memorandum incident, Sullivan was essentially bulletproof. If any new charges were leveled against him, their animus toward Sullivan would be revealed. Everyone knew this unspoken truth. To his credit, Sullivan never gloated about his victory over Nuggle. He kept mostly to himself, with the exception of keeping close counsel with Turley and Conrad. He aced all his remaining exams, as did Turley. They continued to study together until the very last exam.

Every graduating member of NAC 93-03 was allowed no more than three guests for the graduation ceremony. Sullivan invited only his parents, Katerina and John. Katerina stood out with a white flowing dress. John Sullivan wore a brown suit, his only one. FBI Director William Sessions came from Washington to speak to the graduating agents. Everyone sat quietly while the director droned on. His speeches were known for being unremarkable. His tenure as director in general had few highlights. In fact, agents had started calling him “Director Concessions.” As Sullivan listened, he realized the rumors were true. The director was a dud.

Conrad skipped the speech but was waiting in the reception area for Sullivan and his parents when they appeared from the auditorium. Katerina gave Conrad a large motherly hug. Conrad’s mother had died when he was an adolescent, and Katerina had become a surrogate mother to him. He was a frequent presence at the Sullivan supper table. John Sullivan also embraced Conrad.

"You're next, Conrad, right?" he said to the group.

"In two weeks."

"Do you know where you will be assigned, Jimmy?" Katerina asked.

"The lucky bastard is going to Boston." Sullivan poked Conrad in the chest.

"Well, New Haven isn't that far from Bean Town," Conrad answered.

"Yeah, I guess I can't complain. They could have sent me to El Paso."

Turley and his parents came over, and they all introduced themselves. Watching the interaction from the far end of the reception hall was Chris Nuggle. He smirked as he watched them all smiling. He thought back to his phone calls to New Haven. *If they only knew*, he thought.

******

After bidding his parents good-bye and packing his belongings into his car, Sullivan went to the academy's gun vault to retrieve his pistol. He holstered his weapon and walked out of the academy. The August heat in Virginia was stifling. In the short walk to his car, he could already feel the perspiration building on his shirt. As he approached his car, he heard someone behind him.

He turned quickly, gasping in surprise.

"Red. What are you doing here?"

"I was trying to catch you before you left." She smiled.

"Is that right?"

"Yes, I wanted to thank you again. I heard you're going to New Haven. I wanted to wish you luck."

"Well, you're so kind, Red. I should be thanking you."

"Never mind that." Her face reddened. "I'm curious how you knew the thief would return my personal stuff."

"That was easy."

"Tell me."

"The person who took this did it on impulse. She wants to feel she's not a bad person. I just played on that."

"All right, Mr. Mind Reader." She leaned in. "I'm impressed. I hope we'll meet again, young man."

"Me too."

She leaned in and gave him a brief hug and then walked back to the academy. As Sullivan watched her walk away, he thought about her kindness. *How could the same organization that has a Chris Nuggle also have a Melissa Dobson?* he wondered. Perhaps it was nature's way of equalizing things. He pondered this as he drove north toward New England.

TWELVE

Day One

Dalton sat behind his metallic World War II-era desk, a pen tucked in his left ear. Behind him, the light from a large window cast a shadow across the floor in front of his desk. On the wall next to him was his acceptance letter from the FBI, signed by J. Edgar Hoover. Items from the Hoover era had become a novelty item in the FBI. Seated before Dalton was his right hand, Ralph Boreman, and their new agent, Carlos Sullivan. Dalton leaned across his desk and pushed a small black pager toward Sullivan.

"This is your pager," Dalton started. "Don't lose it."

"Yeah," Boreman added, "make sure you keep it on at all times. If you see the office number, call right away."

"Available twenty-four-seven—got it," Sullivan said.

"I suggest you keep an ample supply of quarters with you all the time. You can find a payphone pretty easy around here," Boreman said helpfully.

Dalton looked at Boreman.

"Did you get him wheels?"

"Yep. He'll be driving the gold Chevy Impala."

“Welcome to C-3, Sullivan.” Dalton nodded approvingly. “I’m here if you have any questions. The only thing I ask is that you never lie to me. It’s the most important rule.”

“Understood, sir.”

“Did Boreman mention your first case?” Dalton arched an eye.

“He started briefing me, sir—yes. I’ll be meeting with the detective later this afternoon.”

“Excellent. Listen, kid, you aren’t at the academy anymore. You can call me Tom.”

“Sounds good.” Sullivan rose. He was eager to start his first investigation.

“Okay, kid, go get ’em.” Dalton waved him off.

******

Sullivan was arranging things at his new desk, when he heard footsteps behind him. The floor was uncarpeted, so footfalls were common. Still, they seemed to be approaching him directly. Before he could turn, he heard a female voice.

“Is it true you’re from Boston?”

Sullivan looked her up and down. The smiling girl before him seemed to be no more than twenty years old. He found it curious.

“Medford actually,” he replied.

She extended a hand.

“I’m Trish O’Keefe. I grew up in Lynn. So we’re kind of neighbors.” She beamed.

“I’m Carlos Sullivan.”

“I’m going to work for the FBI one day.”

“So you don’t work here?” Sullivan frowned, confused.

“Oh yes, I’m a summer intern. I’m sorry. Yes, I’m in my final year at UMass Amherst.”

“Oh, now I see.”

“Yeah, the internships in Boston were full. So I found one here in New Haven.”

“Well, you’re very determined.”

“I guess so!” she blurted out.

“You want to be a real crime fighter someday.” He chuckled.

“I’m going to be the best FBI analyst one day.”

“I have no doubt.”

“Well, it was nice meeting you, Carlos Sullivan from Medford.”

O'Keefe walked away beaming, a youthful spring in her step. Once she was gone, Boreman walked over to him and leaned into his ear. He had been watching from the far end of the squad.

"Don't mess with the interns," he whispered angrily.

Before Sullivan could defend himself, Boreman walked off.

*****

Having spoken over the phone, Detective Saucier had asked Sullivan to meet him at a Dunkin' Donuts a few blocks from the Wallingford Police Department. Saucier was not happy at that moment. When he had asked the FBI for help, he was hoping to work with a seasoned agent. Instead, they had offered up a rookie with no experience. It was like a slap in the face. Out of respect for appearances, he agreed to meet with Sullivan, despite his reservations.

Saucier watched from the Dunkin' Donuts' window as Sullivan parked his gold-colored Chevy Impala. It had an unusual black antenna on the car's trunk. It was unmistakably a federal vehicle, at least to the trained eye. Saucier was taken aback at how young Sullivan appeared. He shook his head.

Once Sullivan entered, they shook hands and sat across from each other. After a brief exchange of pleasantries, Saucier started talking about the business at hand. In his left hand, he swirled his coffee.

"Okay, what do you know about the case?"

"Well, I read your letter to the bureau. It was very detailed."

"Good. And thank you."

"Two victims from the same town. Two letters with fingers. One cremation. The remaining fetus had all fingers. No enemies to speak of." Sullivan rattled off the case facts.

"That's about it." Saucier nodded.

"Did the families know each other?"

"No. I thought the same thing."

"Well, I'd like to start by reinterviewing the first victim. Alicia Webster."

"I've already interviewed her."

"I know. But it would help me dive into this if I could speak to her. Do you mind?"

The manner in which Sullivan asked made it impossible for Saucier to object. He assessed the young rookie quickly. First, he had done his homework. Second, he was respectful. Third, he seemed invested in the case. *Check, check, and check*, Saucier thought.

"All right, let's go."

******

Saucier and Sullivan stood outside the front door of the Webster residence within minutes of leaving the Dunkin' Donuts. Saucier's unmarked police cruiser was parked in front. Saucier had agreed to drive. Before knocking on the door, Saucier looked at his young counterpart, placing a hand on his shoulder.

"Remember what this lady's been through."

Sullivan nodded. Saucier rang the doorbell.

After what seemed like five minutes, Alicia Webster answered the door. She had large circles under her eyes. Her face was pale and tired.

"Detective," she said wearily, "how can I help you?"

"Mrs. Webster, I told you I would bring the FBI into the case. This is Agent Sullivan."

Alicia looked at Sullivan incredulously. Sullivan could sense her disbelief.

"I'm Carlos Sullivan," he said. "These are my credentials with the FBI. Can we talk?"

Alicia opened the door fully and waved them in. She ushered them into her kitchen, and they all sat at the table.

"Mrs. Webster, do you work?" Sullivan began.

"I did work. As a secretary in a local law firm. But I quit recently. My husband makes good money, so I'm going to take a break."

"You've had some time to think about this. Have you come up with anyone you think could be behind this?"

"I'm sorry, no. And I don't know the other lady. The one you mentioned to me." She looked over at Saucier.

Sullivan was now having second thoughts about visiting Alicia Webster. She seemed so broken. He sat for a moment, unsure what else to ask. As he stared at the table, he noticed a key chain. It appeared to be her car and home keys. Also attached to the ring was a small plastic card, with an outline of a bicycle for a logo. He found it interesting. He reached out and touched it.

"What is this, Mrs. Webster?"

"Ah, that is my gym pass. Honestly, I stopped going there too."

"I'm sorry to hear that," Sullivan said softly.

"Look, I know the FBI has other cases. I appreciate what you're doing. But I understand if you want to drop this," she said with a defeated air.

"Oh no, Mrs. Webster." He shook his head. "We're going to find who did this."

"You really think so?" she pleaded.

Saucier thought his head was going to explode. He wanted to shake the young rookie. *Stop! Stop!* he thought.

"Absolutely, Mrs. Webster."

Those were the last words spoken as they left the residence. Once they were alone, Saucier stopped the car a block from the Webster house. He looked over at Sullivan.

"Where do you get off making a promise like that?"

"This is my first case. I have every intention of finding the asshole who did this."

"You said *we* would solve this," he glowered.

"If you want, I can go back and tell her I'm only speaking for myself," Sullivan replied.

******

Sullivan was back at his desk an hour later, putting the final touches on his new desk before calling it a day. He had placed a picture of his parents at his college graduation on the right corner of his desk. As he was preparing to go home, Boreman's voice rang out as he approached.

"Sullivan!"

"Yes."

"Come with me. Dalton wants to see you," he ordered.

Once in his supervisor's office, Dalton took over.

"Close the door."

Once the door was closed, Dalton leaned forward in his chair.

"Did you promise a victim that you would solve this case of yours?"

"Not in those words, but yes."

"What were you thinking?" He was practically screaming.

"Look, you took a call from Chris Nuggle at the academy, didn't you?" Sullivan crossed his arms.

Dalton started leaning back slightly. Boreman watched the action without saying a word.

"So what?"

"Thank you for not denying it." He paused. "So he said some unflattering things, and I'm going to prove him wrong."

"Big gamble. You are on probation, kid."

"Look, if I don't solve this case, you won't have to fire me. I'll quit."

*****

Once Sullivan was dismissed, Dalton and Boreman conferred alone, behind a closed door.

"What do you think?"

"I think he might be a loose cannon," Boreman answered sternly.

"Yeah, maybe. Part of me wants to kick him in the balls."

"And the other part of you?"

"The other part wants to give him a pat on the back."

*****

As Sullivan drove home, he thought about the events of his first day as a special agent of the FBI. He had managed to piss off his supervisor and the boss's right hand. Then he had pissed off the detective. He pondered for a moment. *Is there someone I didn't piss off?* Then he thought about the intern. Perhaps, he thought, he had made one friend. The day had a silver lining.

That night, as he lay in bed staring at the ceiling, Sullivan's mind went back in time, to when he was six years old. He remembered the day as if it had been yesterday. He was coming home from school, and his mother was in the kitchen, crying. His dad was leaning against the counter, drunk. A bottle of whiskey was half empty, a glass next to the bottle. For weeks, he had been told that he would soon have a baby brother. He remembered thinking that he would have to share his toys. But this didn't bother him. He would have a brother to play with!

Now Katerina called over to him when she saw him. She was sobbing uncontrollably.

"What's wrong, Mama?"

She wrapped him in her arms tight.

“Oh, Carlito, I’m so sorry. There won’t be a little brother for you.”

He remembers the confusion.

“Why, Mama? Why?” He started to cry in fear.

It was only many years later that he understood what had happened.

As he remembered the incident, he knew he would solve his case. There was no doubt.

THIRTEEN

Trish O'Keefe

New Haven is the second largest city in Connecticut, having been settled in 1638 by English Puritans. It is a coastal city, from which Long Island can be seen on a clear day. Yet it is known more for Yale University and the common area, which has an imprint on its downtown. The New Haven Green, as it is known, is comprised of sixteen acres, much of it shaded by large elm trees. Indeed, the city is known as the Elm City. It was from across the Green that Sullivan sat and waited. From his perch at the Yale Brew, a local coffeehouse, he could see the trees swaying gently in the late August breeze. Sullivan had eaten lunch alone that afternoon, at a deli across from the office. To his surprise, when he returned to his desk, he found a note tucked under his calendar. It read "7:00 p.m. Yale Brew, tonight. Trish."

The note didn't scare him. The author did. He recalled Boreman's warning about associating with the interns. Of course, he had no designs on Trish O'Keefe. She had approached him. This seemed to matter little to Boreman. He was already on thin ice. The last thing he needed was another controversy. Still, he thought it best to meet her. She might have some information.

He looked at his watch impatiently. It was now 7:10 p.m. Just as he prepared to leave the coffee shop, O'Keefe sauntered in the door. She seemed unaware that she was late. Sullivan thought it best not to mention it.

"Sully from Medford, how are you?" she asked, taking a seat next to him.

"I'm intrigued."

"Right. You're wondering why I asked to see you."

"Yes, of course."

"I don't like how you're being treated. I've heard things."

"I see." Sullivan shifted in his seat.

"Have you noticed the other agents on the squad keeping their distance from you?"

"Yeah, I just thought it was a kind of hazing."

"No."

"No?" He scratched his head.

"Boreman has told everyone to keep you at arm's length."

"I'm not surprised."

"How's that?" O'Keefe inquired.

"I had a beef with a supervisor at the academy. I'm sure he's poisoned the well. You've known these guys longer than I have. Any advice?"

"Just keep your head down and do your job. Ignore it."

"I guess."

"How is this case of yours going?"

Sullivan smiled. She was so genuine.

"You want to hear the facts?"

"Sure. Let's hear it." Her smile radiated youthful exuberance.

Sullivan began a recitation of the case facts as he knew them. O'Keefe listened intently. As she listened, at one point she took out a pen and took notes on a small pad.

"Hmmm," she finally interjected as he finished his summary.

"Hmm? That's it?" He laughed.

"I'm thinking."

"I see."

"I'm processing what you've told me. Give me a minute!" she chastised him.

"Okay, Trish from Lynn. Think away." Sullivan crossed his arms and leaned back.

After two solid minutes of silence, she started nodding. She clearly had a thought.

"Did it occur to you that those two women aren't the only victims?" She arched an eye.

"They are the only two to have come forward."

"Sully, this is very sensitive for a woman. There are women who wouldn't want to come forward. They would want it all to go away."

"Why? Wouldn't they want to do something?" he asked, puzzled.

"Miscarriages are delicate. Some women might blame themselves."

"Why would they blame themselves?"

"You're not a woman. You wouldn't understand."

"Maybe you're right."

"Well, if I'm right, those ladies might not be the first or only victims. You should do some digging." She poked him in the chest.

"Digging, yes. I will definitely do some digging." Sullivan smiled but not in a cavalier way. It was a smile of determination.

FOURTEEN

Hospital

After a restless night in bed, Sullivan finally convinced himself to get up. He knew he would not be able to sleep with so much on his mind. The first wisps of morning light were just peeking in through his bedroom blinds. His alarm clock was mercilessly blinking 6:02 a.m. He showered, dressed, and headed to New Haven Medical Center. He put an FBI-laminated placard he had been given on the dash of his car. It read "FBI Official Business" and displayed the FBI seal. He didn't have quarters for the meter, and he hoped the meter maid might bypass him if she saw the placard.

He made his way into the administrative wing of the hospital. He spied a man behind the counter. He appeared to be in his thirties, and he wore a crisp yellow shirt with a name tag. Sullivan read it as he approached the man.

"Hello there, Mr. Nelson."

The man looked up from his newspaper. He held a cup of steaming coffee, which he placed on top of the *New Haven Free Press* when he saw Sullivan.

"How can I help you?"

Sullivan retrieved his credentials and displayed them to the administrator.

"I'm Carlos Sullivan with the FBI. I'm working on the matter involving the miscarriages here at the hospital." Sullivan pointed to his newspaper. "Perhaps you've read about it."

"Yes, people are talking about it here. Very tragic. What can I do?"

"We think that perhaps there are more victims who haven't come forward. Can you check records of other miscarriages prior to these women? Perhaps going back six months?"

Nelson started shaking his head before Sullivan had even finished his question.

"I'm sorry. Patient confidentiality prevents any such disclosure. I wish I could help."

Sullivan was stumped. He knew arguing would be fruitless. Nelson was right.

"Okay, I understand."

Sullivan walked out of the office and down a hallway. He then noticed an arrow on the wall, with the sign "Emergency Room."

*****

Once in the emergency room, Sullivan made inquiries and learned that the head ER nurse was Maggie Flaherty. She was described as in her fifties with gray, shoulder-length hair. More importantly, she was described as "all business." Sullivan took a seat and watched for Nurse Flaherty, hoping for a moment with her. After ten minutes, he saw her near the front desk, talking to a receptionist. He walked over to her.

“Nurse Flaherty?”

“Yes, how can I help you?” she answered helpfully.

“My name is Carlos Sullivan.” He flashed his credentials. “FBI. Can I have a moment?”

Flaherty looked him up and down and then looked at the clock on the wall.

“I have a few minutes,” she answered, ushering him into an empty room.

She closed the door as they entered.

“Thank you for your time,” he started earnestly.

“What’s up?”

“I’m investigating the satanic letters that your patients have received. You must have heard about them.”

“Who here hasn’t? It’s horrible what those women went through. Truly despicable. What can I do to help?”

“I’m checking to verify the true number of victims in this matter.”

“Well, cases of this nature—in young women in particular—are rare.”

“I thought miscarriages were somewhat common?” Sullivan asked.

“Not in the second or third trimester, as in these three women,” Flaherty said confidently.

“Did you say three?”

“Yes, two incidents in the last month, and another two months earlier, that I can recall.”

Sullivan almost jumped out of his skin.

“The first incident, can you tell me about her?”

Flaherty paused. She looked down at the floor and shook her head.

“Ah, you only knew about the last two.” She pointed at him. “Are you tricking me?”

“No, I swear. I admit I didn’t know about that case.”

“I’m not at liberty to discuss that case then, if she hasn’t come forward.” She shook her head resolutely.

“Mrs. Flaherty, I really need your help here. I’m trying to find the creep who’s doing this. He even may work here.” He leaned in.

“Here? Why would you say that?” Her face reddened. She looked out the window, scanning her colleagues walking outside.

“Think about it. The person who did this had to know what happened to these women, had to have access to the fetus, and had to know the personal address of each victim. It makes sense that someone working here fits the bill."

Flaherty stood rigidly, thinking. Her hand went to her face. She realized he was making sense.

"There are confidentiality rules." She hesitated.

Sullivan could tell she wanted to help.

"Look, I won't tell anyone you gave me her name. That's all I need. I won't even tell my bosses."

"I could get in serious trouble." Flaherty shook her head.

"Look, I could get in trouble too. I'm a government agent, asking you to break a rule. It's in my interest to not reveal where I got the name." He looked her straight in the eyes.

Flaherty covered her mouth with her hand, which trembled slightly. She was at a crossroads. The thought of the culprit perhaps working among her staff particularly troubled her. She finally spoke.

"Her name is Heather Knight. She lives in East Haven. That's all I can tell you," she whispered.

"Thank you," Sullivan replied, turning to leave. As he stood at the door, she called out to him.

"Agent Sullivan."

"Yes."

"Good luck."

Sullivan nodded and walked out of the hospital.

In his excitement, Sullivan did not notice Milton Verdun watching him as he walked out of his meeting. Nor did he see Verdun trail him out and take note of his car and license plate.

******

That evening, Sullivan had the FBI night clerk run Heather Knight's driver's-license information, which located her residence in East Haven, Connecticut. It was a second-story apartment in a four-level structure. There were perhaps twenty units in the building. There was no answer at Knight's door, so Sullivan found the superintendent's office on the first floor. The man was in his thirties and sat behind a large wooden desk. Sullivan assessed the man must have weighed at least three hundred pounds. He wore a white, sleeveless T-shirt. Sullivan was certain the building's owner did not use his picture in his rental brochures.

"Can I help you?" the large man asked when Sullivan entered the office.

"Sure, what's your name?"

"I'm Todd Armstrong, the superintendent."

"Excellent, I'm Carlos Sullivan, FBI. I'm looking for Heather Knight. Do you know where I can find her?" Sullivan asked, displaying his credentials.

"Is she in trouble?" Todd put down a large 7-Eleven Big Gulp, which he had been cradling in his left hand.

"Not at all. I just need to speak with her."

"She went away for a week. She mentioned her parents in Florida. Come back next week."

"Here's my card"—Sullivan placed it on Todd's desk—"so you can let me know when she returns."

"Sure, I guess."

"Thanks."

Frustrated, Sullivan walked out of the office. On the positive side, he thought, a week gave him time to confer with Detective Saucier and strategize.

FIFTEEN

Game Changer

Paula White drove to her doctor's office with a sense of trepidation. Dr. Shoptrain's administrative assistant had called her home, asking her to come and see the doctor immediately. When she asked to speak to him on the phone, the administrator insisted that the doctor wanted to see her in person. Almost two weeks had passed since her miscarriage. Perhaps the meeting concerned the blood work the doctor had ordered. *What else could it be?* she wondered.

She hurriedly walked into the doctor's office. Before she could even say boo to the administrator, she was waved to the window. The administrator slid the glass door open quickly and called Mrs. White over.

"Please, I'll buzz you in," she said, pointing to the side door.

Once inside, the administrator walked her to a small examination room.

"Have a seat. Dr. Shoptrain will be right with you."

White did as instructed. She was practically crawling out of her skin. The drama was too much for her. *This had better be important*, she thought. After what seemed like an eternity but what was in reality only two minutes, Dr. Shoptrain stepped into the office.

He swung a seat around and sat down next to White.

"Paula," he started, "I've got the blood work back." His tone was serious.

"I knew it!" She put a hand to her face. "What is wrong?"

"Were you taking heavy doses of vitamin D?" he asked, putting a hand on her shoulder.

"I took a vitamin supplement. I assume it has vitamin D."

"No, that supplement would not have such a high level of vitamin D," he said sternly.

"Can that cause a miscarriage?" She gasped.

"A high enough concentration could, especially if mixed with other substances."

"What are you saying?"

"I also found traces of phosphates."

"Could this have caused what happened?" She was terrified.

"Possibly, except this blood work was taken three days after your incident." White avoided being more clinical.

"What does this mean?"

"I can't say definitively. Given that this blood work was taken late. I blame myself for that. But this could mean that you were poisoned."

White was stunned. She sat silently, her hand covering her mouth.

“Poisoned?” she finally muttered.

“Perhaps it was accidental. Did you have an exterminator at your house recently?”

“No. Not at all…” She hesitated. “An exterminator?”

“These elements are what you might expect to find in some rat poisons.”

White sat, thinking. She started composing herself.

“I knew this wasn’t right. I knew it!” She stood up.

“Paula, we don’t know it was intentional.” Dr. Shoptrain stood up as well.

“So whether intentional or not, the poison could have caused the miscarriage, Doctor?”

“Yes, Paula, possibly yes.”

A tear welled in her eye as she sat down again.

*****

That afternoon, Sullivan received a call from Detective Saucier, asking him to meet at the police station. He told Sullivan there was a development. When Sullivan inquired about the nature of the development, Saucier was typically blunt.

"I have no clue, kid. Come and we'll find out together. Paula White has summoned us."

After parking his Gold Impala in the police visitors' lot, Sullivan noticed that Saucier was already in the parking lot, standing next to his parked unmarked cruiser.

"Am I late?" Sullivan asked.

"No, I'm just anxious to see what Mrs. White has to say."

"Was she okay?"

"I guess, but she sounded very intense."

"I see."

Sullivan jumped in Detective Saucier's car, and they started toward the White residence. As they did so, Sullivan recounted how he had discovered a third recent miscarriage at the hospital. He explained that Heather Knight was out of town but that he would follow up on this lead. Saucier nodded as Sullivan spoke.

"How did you get the girl's name?" Saucier looked over.

"It's better I don't say."

"You feds crack me up. All right, run with it. It is interesting."

When they arrived at White's front door, they didn't have to knock. Brian White opened the door as their feet hit the landing. He ushered them in with a wave of his hand.

"Thanks for coming," he said.

"Of course, Mr. White," Saucier replied.

At the kitchen table, they observed Mrs. White, her two-year-old boy bouncing in her lap. They could tell she had been crying. As she said nothing at first, Saucier and Sullivan helped themselves to seats at the table.

"You asked to see us, Mrs. White," Saucier started.

"Do you see my boy, Nicholas?"

Saucier and Sullivan looked at each other.

"We do, Mrs. White."

Her face reddened as she looked back at them.

"Well, he would have had a baby sister today. Except his little sister was murdered." Her voice was flat, lifeless.

"Murdered?" Sullivan inquired.

"I was poisoned!" she screamed. Her husband rushed over and scooped up baby Nicholas. He hurriedly walked to the living room.

"Mrs. White, how do you know this?" Saucer asked.

"My doctor did blood work! I was poisoned!" Her screams were louder now.

"What kind of poison?" Sullivan interjected.

"Rat poison, most likely! What the fuck does it matter what kind of poison!"

"Do you have the lab report?" Saucier inquired.

She reached across the table and found the report the doctor had given her. She threw it at them.

"Here's the fucking lab report! It's all yours." She started sobbing.

Saucier looked across the room, over at Brian White, pleading for an intervention.

Mr. White took the clue and came to console his wife. He walked her back to their bedroom, while baby Nicholas peered from a playpen in the living room.

"Mr. White, we will look into this. Given that we have other victims. We may now be looking at a serial."

Brian White turned pale.

"Like a serial killer?"

"Yeah, like that." Saucier stared at him. "We'll be in touch."

Once they were both outside, Sullivan shook his head in disbelief. Saucier nodded in silent agreement.

"This is a game changer, kid."

*****

That evening, Sullivan was bouncing off the walls, as if he had downed twelve cups of coffee. He could barely contain himself. What at first appeared to be a case of a deranged person might actually be murder, perhaps even multiple homicides. While murder in and of itself did not fall under FBI jurisdiction, the letter portion of the case gave him cause to continue in the assignment. He thought of Trish O'Keefe and dialed her at home.

She picked up on the second ring.

Sullivan excitedly recounted the events of the previous days. The first unreported stillbirth, the elusive Heather Knight, and then the poison found in Mrs. White's blood. O'Keefe listened without interruption. Finally, Sullivan realized she was silent.

"Are you still there?"

"Yes, Sully, I'm listening."

"Don't you have anything to say?"

"Well, I would say I told you so."

"Right, about the unreported miscarriage. I thought you were beyond saying 'I told you so'?"

"No, not really." He could feel her smiling into the phone.

"I have a friend you should meet. He's graduating from the academy on Monday."

"What's his name?"

"Jimmy Conrad. You'd like him. He's from Boston."

"Interesting."

"Yeah, he's like a brother."

"Well, I look forward to meeting him."

"So do you have any more tips for me?" He smiled.

"Well, I would say you need to track down Ms. Knight. That will be huge."

"That I know. Anything else?"

"Yeah, I would keep Dalton in the loop. He doesn't like surprises."

"Good advice, Trish from Lynn."

There was a pause in their conversation.

"Well, it's late," Sullivan finally interjected. "I hope I'm not annoying you."

"No way, Sully. I want to help any way I can. Don't you dare cut me out!" she scolded.

After they hung up, it took Sullivan two hours to finally fall asleep.

SIXTEEN

Roadblocks

The next morning, Sullivan was at his desk working on a written time line. He thought that laying out all the facts in sequence might help him focus on new leads. He also decided to heed O'Keefe's advice. He watched for Dalton's arrival so he could brief him on the new developments. It was 9:00 a.m., and Dalton was still not in. The door to his office was open, and his light was off. Just outside the door, sitting and reading some reports, was Boreman. His desk was just outside of Dalton's office, almost as if he were guarding the door. Even the secretary, Sandra Toulouse, sat farther away.

Thirty minutes later, Dalton walked into the squad area and straight into his office. He waved at Sandra and nodded at Boreman as he did so. Before Dalton could sit down, Boreman walked in after him. Sullivan watched and decided it best to wait. After Boreman finished his meeting with Dalton, he went right back to his desk. Sullivan saw an opportunity and walked toward his supervisor's office.

"Hold on, rookie." Boreman put his hand up.

"What?" Sullivan asked, irritated.

"Where are you going?"

"I was going to talk to my supervisor; what does it look like?"

"Are you a smartass now?" Boreman's voice level went up a notch.

"I don't mean to be."

"So it just comes naturally?"

"When I'm asked a stupid question, yeah."

Boreman rose from his chair. Sullivan stood defiantly. He was not backing down.

"Well, you can't see him now. He's busy."

"Is he the pope?" Sullivan asked, annoyed.

"Yeah, and I'm the Swiss guard," Boreman retorted.

Inside his office, Dalton could hear the exchange. He was enjoying Sullivan sticking up for himself. At the same time, he was curious about Boreman's animosity. He decided to say nothing, for now.

Dalton watched from his chair as Sullivan shook his head and walked off in disgust.

*****

Realizing he was wasting time in the squad area, Sullivan decided to pay Alicia Webster a visit. She was the first reported victim. Sullivan had already discussed this visit with Saucier, who was busy with other cases. He gave Sullivan the green light. The rookie was growing on him.

“Go ahead, kid,” Sullivan recalled him saying. “Run with it.”

He now sat across from Webster at her kitchen table.

“Have you found the person who did this?” she asked.

“Not yet, Mrs. Webster.”

“You promised me you would find the person,” she reminded him.

Sullivan was painfully aware of the consequences of that promise. He gulped.

“Yes, Mrs. Webster. I will find the person.”

“All right,” she said, “go on.”

“I just need to know if you had any blood work done after your incident, either at the hospital or after.”

“No, I’m sorry. Why?”

“The other victim, we think she was poisoned. Did you drink anything unusual just prior to your incident?” Sullivan kept referring to the miscarriage euphemistically.

“Are you saying I was poisoned?” Her face contorted.

“Without a lab report, we may never know.”

“Oh no.” Her shoulders slumped.

“What did you do prior to the incident?”

"I went to the gym that morning."

"Hmm," Sullivan said softly. "That gym?" Sullivan pointed to her key chain, with the bicycle logo.

"Yeah, the Cycle Center."

"I see. Did you drink or eat anything?"

"Just water, at the gym."

"Did you vomit during the incident?"

"Yes, actually, I did. I was poisoned, wasn't I?" She gasped.

Sullivan knew that rat poison caused vomiting in humans. Rats cannot vomit, which is why it is so lethal to them. Although rat poison rarely caused death in an adult, it could wreak havoc on a fetus. Still, he had no proof. He thought it best to measure his words.

"Mrs. Webster, I'm still investigating. Let's not jump to conclusions." He rose to leave.

She walked him to the door. As he was leaving, she called out to him.

"Agent Sullivan."

"Yes, Mrs. Webster."

"Don't forget your promise." Tears welled in her eyes as she held the door open.

"I won't. You have my word."

******

That afternoon, as the late September sun started its usual descent toward the horizon, Sullivan drove to Heather Knight's apartment building. Having driven by the two previous days also, he had ascertained which window corresponded to her residence. Rather than appear like a stalker and visit the superintendent again, he decided to spot-check for any activity. He parked his Impala strategically so he could watch her window. The blinds to her kitchen window were open, as were the curtains in her bedroom. He waited an hour. He saw no movement or lights. It was obvious she was still away. *Another roadblock*, he thought.

Sullivan was tempted to drive his bureau car to Florida right then and there to track her down. He imagined what Boreman would do if acted on such an impulse. *Most likely have a heart attack*, he thought. As he pulled away from Knight's building, Sullivan wondered what he had done to earn the hostility coming from Boreman. He pledged to himself, on his honor, he would not let anyone stand in his way. With that solemn conviction, he drove into the descending darkness.

SEVENTEEN

Conspiracy

Later that evening, Gerald McCormick was still at work, finishing up some paperwork for his father. His apprenticeship was coming along nicely. In due time, his father said he would be running the McCormick's Funeral Home. His tenure would represent the fourth generation of McCormicks to operate the funeral business. And a business it was. Every detail of the burial process came at a cost. A cost that the McCormicks were ready to explain in detail to every grieving customer. The explanation was done in an empathetic way, with soft hushed tones, such that the customer ended up thinking it was their idea after all, to have a hermetically sealed coffin, made of the most durable design. Gerald was a natural salesman. He had a silver tongue and the demeanor of a consoling preacher.

His father had already left earlier in the afternoon. It was left to Gerald to lock up. He always thought it was a curious exercise. *Who would want to break into a funeral home?* he thought. As he walked down the wooden front steps to the parking lot, he saw a figure leaning against his car. He stopped, frozen. Then he cautiously started walking toward the vehicle. He could now identify the person against his car. *Damn*, he whispered quietly.

"Milt, what the hell are you doing here?"

"Did you forget us, Gerry?" Milton's face was red, angry.

"Of course not!" he whispered, conspiratorially.

"We've asked for a meeting. Where have you been?"

"I have a business to run, as you can see."

"Oh, and I'm just a hospital orderly, right?"

"I didn't say that, Milt. I said that we should lay low for a while. Until everything blows over."

"Well, we may have a problem." Milton leaned in.

"What is it?"

"The detective from town, Saucier, he is really looking into this. On top of that, the FBI is now involved! There's an agent; he's young. He's been snooping around," Milton hissed.

"You guys turned this into a federal case, for Christ's sake. You enjoyed it too much," Gerald fired back.

"We did you a favor." Milton pointed at him, accusingly.

"Yes, and you will be compensated. We're friends, remember?"

"You'd better not let us down."

"I won't." Gerald looked around. He saw nobody.

"What do we do about those cops?"

"We won't do anything. Are you crazy? This will die down. Just lay low. I'll be in touch."

“We will wait, Gerry, but not forever.”

With that admonition, Milton Verdun turned and walked off into the darkness. As Gerald watched him ominously disappear, a shiver came over him.

EIGHTEEN

Interview

The next morning Sullivan sat at his desk, wearily eyeing Dalton's door. He had arrived early that morning, hoping to catch an audience with his supervisor before Boreman could stop him. Once again, however, he was disappointed. Dalton was not in. He knew Dalton was a serious person and a professional. His absence merely meant he was at a meeting elsewhere, perhaps with another law-enforcement agency. The reason for his absence mattered little to Sullivan. He just wanted to have a few minutes alone with his boss.

Before Sullivan could even contemplate his next move, Boreman arrived, a steaming cup of coffee in one hand and a newspaper tucked under his other arm. He looked over at Sullivan, seemingly sneering. For his part, Sullivan pretended not to see him. An uncomfortable silence hung over the squad room. Three other agents sat at their desks; none of them made eye contact with Sullivan. It seemed as if Boreman had given them their marching orders.

The squad silence was pierced with the ringing of Sullivan's desk phone. He picked up the receiver quickly.

"This is Sullivan," he answered.

Boreman strained to hear the other party but could not.

"This is Todd. The super. You asked me to call you."

"Is she back?" Sullivan interrupted.

"Yes, she got back this morning. Should I tell her you're coming—?"

"Don't say a word. I'm on my way."

Sullivan slapped the phone down, stood up, and grabbed his jacket, which was draped over his chair. Boreman put his coffee down and appeared about to say something, when Sullivan gave him a "Don't fuck with me" glare. In an instant, Sullivan was gone.

*****

Before climbing the stairs to Heather Knight's apartment, Sullivan stopped at the super's office and passed him a twenty-dollar bill. The gesture was gratefully accepted. Sullivan had noticed that Todd was wearing the same stained T-shirt. *Maybe now he'll get a new T-shirt*, Sullivan thought, as it dawned on him that the rotund building manager had become his first informant.

Once at Knight's door, he rapped twice. There was no doorbell. After two or three minutes, Sullivan was starting to get anxious. Then he heard movement. In another instant, the door swung open. A young female leaned against the doorframe, staring at Sullivan.

"Can I help you?" she asked impatiently.

Sullivan noticed that Heather was in her early twenties; yet she possessed a sad quality that made her seem ten years older. She had dark bags under her eyes. Her dark hair had wisps of silver, which was unusual in a young lady; it was tied in a bun. She stared at Sullivan, waiting for an answer.

"I'm Carlos Sullivan, special agent with the FBI," he replied, displaying his credentials.

"Oh." Her eyes widened. "What does the FBI want with me?"

"May I come in?"

She hesitated for a second. Then she swung the door wide open. "Come on in." She waved him in.

"Just don't judge me on the apartment, Agent Sullivan."

"You can call me Carlos."

Sullivan scanned the small apartment and could see what she meant. There were empty pizza boxes on the kitchen table. Fast-food bags were crunched up around the couch. And discarded soda cans littered the living-room floor. Heather walked him to the kitchen, grabbed the pizza boxes, and placed them on the counter. She motioned to a seat at the small table.

"Is this okay?"

"That's great, Ms. Knight."

"Heather is okay."

Sullivan put his hands on the table and settled in. He paused for effect, giving her a serious look.

"I'm here about what happened to you."

Heather looked up at the ceiling. Her eyes reddened as she fought back tears.

"You're here about my stillbirth?" she finally responded.

"Yes."

Tears were now streaming down her face. Sullivan got up and got some napkins he noticed on the counter, handing them to her.

"But you're with the FBI."

"It might seem confusing."

"Yeah, you can say that!" She wiped her tears.

"Have you heard about the other women who also had miscarriages?"

"No. I've been away a lot."

"You didn't see this in the news?"

She waved her right hand across the room like a wand. "Does it look like I read the news?"

"I see." He continued, "There have been two other cases since yours. I'm looking into the possibility—"

"That this wasn't an accident!" she interrupted, practically screaming.

"Yes, possibly, that's what I'm investigating."

"Oh my God," she said, "I don't even know what to feel right now."

"I have some questions."

"Sure," she answered as she continued wiping her tears.

"I have to ask. Who was the baby's father?"

Upon hearing this question, her face reddened, and she started rocking slightly in her chair.

"I thought he cared about me. We dated for two years. He didn't want anything to do with the baby. He even said, 'How do I know it's mine?'"

Both hands covered her face as she stared at the floor.

"His name, Heather?"

"Gerald McCormick."

Sullivan started scanning his mind upon hearing the name; it seemed so familiar. Then he recalled the detective's reports.

"Gerald McCormick. From the funeral home?"

"Yeah, that's the bastard. Kind of ironic, isn't it?"

"That's not the word I was thinking actually." Then he thought for a moment.

"Did his funeral home handle the arrangements?"

"He offered, the son of a bitch. He left me a cold voice mail. He actually sounded relieved. I wanted nothing to do with him. My parents helped me…arranged another place for the service."

Heather seemed to regain some of her composure as they continued talking. She placed the napkins on the table and looked up at Sullivan.

"Do you think he did this to me?"

"I'm working on this, Heather, but we can't let him know we're looking into this yet. Does that make sense?"

"Yeah, it does." She shook her head. "Don't worry; I haven't talked to him since I lost my baby. He never even came to visit me after."

Sullivan gave her another serious look.

"Did you get a letter?"

Heather looked at him in amazement. The blood rushed from her head. She said nothing but got up and walked to her bedroom. A moment later, she returned with a letter in her hand. She handed it to Sullivan.

"I got this in the mail a week later. I thought that it might be Gerry. Who else?"

"Did you confront him about it?"

"Fuck no. I wouldn't give him the satisfaction."

Sullivan looked at the letter carefully. The wording and style were almost identical to the others.

"Does it look like his handwriting?"

"It's block lettering. I don't remember what his writing was like. It's not like the asshole ever sent me a love letter."

"I'm going to have to take the letter."

"Yeah, I was actually going to toss it. As you can see, I'm not a neat freak." She finally cracked a smile.

"Heather, was there anything in the letter?"

"Like what?"

"Never mind," Sullivan answered, realizing her answer was sufficient.

"So will you tell me if Gerry did this to me, once you know?" She put a hand on Sullivan's arm.

"I promise I will."

"Okay, thanks." She got up and walked Sullivan to the door.

Before walking out, Sullivan turned to her.

"One last question, Heather."

"Shoot."

"Did you belong to a gym?"

"Yeah, but I haven't gone back since this happened."

"Let me guess. Was it the Cycle Center?"

"Yeah, how did you know that?"

"I'm with the FBI. We know things." He smiled.

NINETEEN

Chess

The clock on Supervisor Dalton's wall clock indicated it was 2:57 p.m., and Boreman was fuming. Steam was practically coming out of his ears. Earlier that afternoon, Dalton had called Boreman into his office for a quick meeting. As he now sat across from Dalton, waiting, Boreman replayed the conversation in his head.

"Ralph, can you come in here?"

"What's up, boss?"

"It seems like the rookie is making progress on his case. And it appears to be more serious than we thought initially."

"What? How's that?"

"It may be that these girls were poisoned. Further,"—Dalton pointed into the air for emphasis—"he found a potential motive. It may not be demonic crap. He thinks it was a guy who did this to his pregnant girlfriend. The other letters may have been meant as some sort of distraction, according to Sullivan."

"How do you know this?" Boreman was puzzled, having blocked Sullivan's meetings with his boss.

"Detective Saucier called me. He and Sullivan are asking for a meeting. At three p.m. Can you join us?"

"I wouldn't miss it."

Boreman walked out in a barely concealed rage. The rookie had outmaneuvered him. *That's not the end of this chess match,* he thought at the time. A few hours later, he was back in Dalton's office, waiting with his boss, his feet tapping the floor quietly.

At 3:00 p.m. exactly, Sullivan escorted Saucier into the office. Dalton rose and greeted Saucier heartily. Boreman remained seated, brooding, his blood boiling, arms crossed.

"John, it's been way too long. It's good to see you," Dalton said warmly.

"'Same, Tim; we need to get a beer sometime, soon."

"Absolutely."

"So I wanted to thank you for assigning Sullivan here to help me." Saucier looked over at the rookie with a wry smile.

"Honestly, we had some hiccups in the beginning, but he's doing a good job."

Sullivan sat quietly, observing. He thought it best to let Saucier speak.

"So what else can we do?" Dalton asked.

"Why don't I let Sullivan brief you? He broke these new leads." He put a hand on Sullivan's shoulder.

As he watched the meeting, a vein began to throb in Boreman's forehead. He was turning red. It did not escape Dalton's notice.

"Sir—" Sullivan began.

"Cut that out, Sully," Dalton interrupted.

"Okay, boss. I think that this was orchestrated by Gerald McCormick. He is the heir to the McCormick's Funeral Home."

"I know the father; he's a good man," Saucier said, "but I can't speak to the son."

"Go on."

"Well, his girlfriend was Heather Knight. She also received a letter but never reported it. I have that letter now, and I put it in evidence with the others. We also have the toxicology report from Paula White, indicating she may have been poisoned." Sullivan was getting animated as he recited his theory.

"So what's the connection?" Dalton asked.

"The victims all attended the same gym. The Cycle Center. I think that is where they were poisoned."

"Does McCormick also work at the gym?" Boreman interrupted skeptically.

"No. I'm piecing that together."

"So you have nothing," Boreman emphasized.

“Not yet obviously. But we have a plan.”

“What’s that?” Dalton inquired.

“I’d like to get a grand jury subpoena for McCormick’s handwriting. Maybe we’ll get lucky,” Sullivan said.

“Or maybe not,” Boreman interjected. “Handwriting analysis is usually a waste of time.”

“What could it hurt?” Sullivan shrugged his shoulders.

“Well, once you slap him with a subpoena, you’ll be tipping off McCormick that he’s your suspect,” Dalton said, scratching his head.

“We’ve thought of that. Detective Saucier and I think even if there is no match, it might shake the trees. He’ll get nervous and make a mistake.”

Saucier said nothing but nodded in agreement. The room went quiet for a moment. Finally, Dalton broke the silence.

“Run with it, kid. It’s your case!” Dalton rose.

Sullivan and Saucier both stood up. Boreman remained seated.

“Thanks for hearing me out on my case, boss.” Sullivan beamed, looking over at Boreman.

Dalton smiled but said nothing further. He realized what Sullivan was doing.

As Sullivan and Saucier walked out, Boreman followed closely behind them. Once Saucier was out in the hallway, he stepped in front of Sullivan, pointing a finger at him.

"Don't think you can fuck with me, kid!" he raged.

"I don't know what you're talking about."

"I'm watching you!"

Sullivan shrugged his shoulders in a carefree way, further enraging Boreman.

"Excuse me," Sullivan said, stepping around him, "I've got things to do."

From across the squad room, Dalton had watched his primary agent scolding the rookie, and frowned. *What am I missing?* he wondered.

TWENTY

AUSA

The US attorneys' office was located in the Richard C. Lee United States Courthouse, directly across the street from the New Haven Green, and just a few short steps from the FBI office. From his office, Assistant US Attorney (AUSA) Steve Kaplan could not see the famous park. He had only been an AUSA for three years, so his view consisted of an alleyway from the side of the building. But he didn't take the job for the money or the perks, because there were none. He did the job out of a sense of duty to his country. His goal was to become the most respected federal prosecutor in Connecticut. For now, however, he would have to settle for listening to FBI rookies, much like he was probably viewed by the other senior prosecutors.

He checked his watch. It was already 9:00 a.m., and his appointment was not yet there. After scheduling the appointment, Kaplan had asked the other prosecutors, "Has anyone here worked with Special Agent Carlos Sullivan?" The answer was a unanimous *no*. He was an unknown quantity. At exactly 9:01 a.m., Sullivan knocked on Kaplan's door, which was open.

Immediately, Kaplan was taken by how young Sullivan appeared.

"Come on in," he said, rising and shaking Sullivan's hand.

"Thanks for seeing me."

“Of course, Agent Sullivan.”

“You can call me Sully.”

“All right, and I’m just Steve.”

“Cool.”

Sullivan sat down and spent fifteen minutes laying out his case. After he was done, Sullivan reached over and placed laminated photos of all three letters on his desk. A second set of photos showed the letters in ziplock bags, sealed with evidence tape. Finally, he placed a Xerox copy of each letter on the desk for him to retain.

“I take it fingerprints were negative?” Kaplan asked.

“Correct, we found some, but nothing that was in the system. Most likely the postal workers.”

“I see,” he said, inspecting the evidence.

Kaplan read each letter carefully. Then he put them down.

“So you are thinking of getting handwriting exemplars?” Kaplan asked.

“Samples, yes.”

“From McCormick?”

“Yes.”

“I like the motive factor. He has a strong motive. Have you considered that state charges might be stronger?”

"I'm working with a local detective. State charges aren't out of the question, but for now, I really would like to hit him with a federal subpoena."

Kaplan nodded his head.

"You might have something here. I can get you a grand jury subpoena. I'll present this to them this afternoon."

"So fast?"

"Sure. Come by tomorrow morning and pick it up."

"How does this work?" Sullivan asked. "I'm new at this."

"The subpoena will compel him to provide writing exemplars. If he does not cooperate, he can be hit with other charges."

"So I can make him write what I want?"

"Yes and no. You will dictate the letters to him. Obviously, you don't want him to see the letters. He'll have to write exactly what's on these as you read them to him. And you can have him write it multiple times."

Sullivan was taking notes.

"What if he asks for a lawyer?"

"The lawyer can be present but can't interfere."

"Cool." Sullivan smiled.

He stood up and shook Kaplan's hand strongly.

“Thank you, Steve.”

Kaplan smiled as Sullivan briskly left the office, taken in by the kid’s enthusiasm.

TWENTY- ONE

Betrayal

Dalton sat alone in his office. He sat pensively, gazing out his window. The day had been overcast, and the sun appeared to be setting a bit earlier each night. Everyone had left for home, but Dalton remained, and he was troubled. He was aware that new agents are usually subjected to pranks or light hazing, but what he had witnessed was too much. Some new agents would sit down in their chair, for instance, only to flop to the ground because the bolts had been undone. Other times, senior agents made the rookies wash their cars. This situation between Boreman and Sullivan, however, seemed personal.

Then he considered how Sullivan had been poorly recommended by Chris Nuggle, an agent at Quantico, whom Dalton had never met. While the rookie had made a couple of missteps, and he was cocky, he was by all accounts doing a good job. He liked the kid's enthusiasm.

Dalton fiddled with his Rolodex until he found the card he was looking for. Jim Dawson, instructor at the FBI Academy. He had met Dawson three years previously at an FBI training, and they had hit it off. On the back of the card, Dawson had written his home number. It was 7:15 p.m. *Perhaps*, he thought, *Dawson might be home.*

"Good evening." Dawson picked up the phone after several rings.

"Dawson, it's Tim Dalton. How are you?"

"Tim, long time, no hear."

"Very true. Next time I'm in Virginia, we need to get together."

"Sounds good. What can I do for you?"

"I have a rookie here. Do you remember a student called Carlos Sullivan?"

"Sully, yeah. He made some waves here I guess. He's very smart. I kind of liked him."

"I see." He paused. "Well, I got a call from Chris Nuggle; he works at the academy also. Do you know him?"

"Of course. His office is right around the corner. He really had a beef with Sullivan. Tried to get him booted."

"What's this Nuggle like?"

"You're kidding, right?" Dawson was puzzled.

"No, why?"

"Why don't you ask Boreman? Isn't he your primary?"

Dalton gulped. His heart sank.

"What do you mean?"

"Boreman and Nuggle are tight. He was Nuggle's best man at his wedding. He can tell you all you want to know about Nuggle."

“I see.” Dalton was feeling sick.

“Hey, listen; I won’t mention this to Nuggle,” Dawson said, realizing what had happened.

“I appreciate that, Jim. Thank you.”

Dalton hung up the phone, shaking his head in disgust. He recalled every instance when a new agent would arrive on his squad. It had become a ritual. Each time, his one and only mantra was always “Don’t ever lie to me.” How many times had Boreman sat next to him when he had laid down Dalton’s law? Now Boreman’s denial echoed in his ears.

“Do you know Nuggle?” Dalton recalled asking.

“Nope, never,” he had answered.

His first impulse was to order Boreman into the office right then and there. But he decided to take a different course. He would wait.

*****

Gerald McCormick was finishing up some paperwork in his father’s office, when the phone rang. It was late, and the business was closed. *Who could it be?* he wondered.

“This is Gerry,” he said, mildly annoyed.

“It’s Tony. From East Haven, remember me?”

“Yeah, I remember.”

"You gave me a hundred-dollar bill and asked me to keep an eye on your girl."

"You have news about Heather?"

"Yeah, real important news," he emphasized.

"All right, I have another Benjamin here for you. What do you have?"

"She was out of town, like I told you. But she came back, and the FBI paid her a visit."

"The FBI?" McCormick's heart skipped a beat.

"Yeah. Agent Carlos Sullivan."

"He's young, right?" McCormick thought back to what Milton had told him.

"Yes, midtwenties. He spent a lot of time with your girl."

McCormick was frozen for a moment. He said nothing. After a few seconds, Tony spoke again.

"When can I get my money?"

"You know where I work. I'll leave it with the secretary."

"All right."

"Thanks, Tony," he said, hanging up the phone.

McCormick thought of his options. This was not good news. *Perhaps*, he thought, *I should convene a meeting*.

TWENTY-TWO

Subpoena

Conrad had just settled comfortably into a brown leather recliner in his new apartment in South Boston, when his phone rang. He didn't want to get up, but only two people had his new number. The first was the landlord, with whom he had spoken only a few hours earlier. The second person was Sullivan. Earlier, Sullivan had called him at the academy to apologize for not being able to attend his graduation. He hadn't accumulated any annual leave in his short FBI tenure. Further, Boreman was unlikely to grant him any favors. More to the point, Sullivan explained that he didn't want to ask Boreman and give him the satisfaction of shooting him down.

As Conrad reached for the phone, he already knew who it was.

"Sully," he said into the phone.

"Hey, Jimmy, how's your new place in Southie?"

"I think I'll like it."

"I'm hoping to come home for Thanksgiving. I can check it out then."

"I'll have beers on ice."

"I'm really sorry I couldn't make your graduation."

"I know, brother; don't give it another thought. Are we still on for tomorrow?"

"Yes, I just need your pager number."

Conrad fiddled with his notebook, looking for the number. He hadn't had time to memorize it yet. He read it to Sullivan, and their conversation was over. There was no need for further small talk.

*****

Gerald McCormick arrived at the FBI office, escorted by his father, Michael McCormick, and their attorney, Jeremiah Benson. Attorney Benson carried an overstuffed leather briefcase. They wore dark expensive suits and serious grimaces. They looked as though they were in the middle of a funeral mass. The irony did not escape Sullivan, who suppressed a smile. He greeted them briefly in the reception area and escorted them into a conference room. Detective Saucier was already waiting in the conference room.

As they walked to the room, Sullivan thought back to the cool manner in which Gerald had taken the subpoena from him a day earlier. He didn't protest or complain. In fact, it seemed as though he had been expecting a visit. His demeanor only cemented Sullivan's opinion that he was on the right track. An innocent person would have asked questions.

As they took seats around the conference table, Sullivan pointed to Saucier at the end of the table.

“This is Detective Saucier,” Sullivan announced. The guests nodded in his direction.

Benson opened the meeting.

“Mr. Sullivan, I want to make it clear that my client will not be making any statements or taking any questions.”

“That’s fine. The subpoena is for handwriting exemplars only.”

“What exactly is this about?” McCormick senior asked.

“Why don’t you ask your son?” Sullivan answered.

“I have no idea what this is about,” Gerald interrupted.

“Gerald McCormick is a person of interest in a case involving threatening letters.” Sullivan looked at the elder McCormick.

“This is outrageous,” he answered, placing his hands on the table for emphasis.

“Dad, don’t worry. I haven’t done anything wrong. Let’s just get this over with.”

“Great idea; let’s get started,” Sullivan commanded.

He then placed a pen and a pad of paper in front of Gerald.

“You will use these to write what I dictate.”

“Whatever,” he replied.

“Okay,” Sullivan said, “let’s begin. Write the following: ‘Alicia, your womb belongs to Satan. You belong to him alone. Your little girl is with him now.’”

“I don’t even know an Alicia!” Gerald grimaced.

“Please comply.”

Benson leaned over and whispered something into Gerald’s ear. He then picked up his pen and began writing.

When he hesitated, Sullivan repeated the statement.

Sullivan and Saucier watched as Gerald wrote the statement ten times. Then they dictated the letter received by Paula White. This was followed by Heather’s letter, which started with her name. Sullivan raised his voice slightly and looked right at McCormick as he read the last missive. The entire procedure took no more than thirty minutes. When they concluded, Benson reached over and handed Sullivan and Saucier his business card.

“You are to have no further contact with my client.”

Sullivan said nothing but smiled at Gerald, in an attempt to get under his skin.

They all rose, and Sullivan escorted them out of the office.

As soon as the McCormicks and their lawyer were out of FBI space, Sullivan walked quickly back to his squad room, followed closely by Saucier. He inspected the exemplars as they reached Sullivan’s desk. He shook his head as Sullivan reached for his phone and dialed a number, after which he input several digits.

"I hate to tell you, kid, but this is a bust. These samples look nothing like the letters."

"It doesn't matter."

"Doesn't matter?" Saucier held up the samples in his hand.

"We're shaking the tree, remember?"

"Yeah, I know. I'm just disappointed."

Boreman, who was listening from his desk, walked over to them.

"I told you this was a waste of time, Sullivan."

"I don't think so."

Sullivan pulled Saucier away and walked with him out of the squad area. Saucier was a visitor at the FBI, so he didn't think it was his place to say anything to Boreman. In fact, he had only met him once before, at his previous meeting with Dalton. However, once they were outside of earshot, he couldn't resist. Saucier leaned over slightly and whispered, "Who's the asshole?"

TWENTY-THREE

Surveillance

Conrad was parked diagonally from the FBI office, sitting in his newly assigned bureau car, a dark-blue Ford Taurus with Massachusetts plates. In one hand, he held a pair of binoculars, and in the other, a map of central Connecticut. He had studied it as best he could in the limited time available. Lying in the seat next to him was a Nikon camera with a zoom lens, which he had signed out of the office.

After reporting for duty in Boston, Conrad was assigned to a violent-crimes task force. He had been embraced like a returning prodigal son by his squad mates and his supervisor. They didn't blink when he asked to help a fellow agent in the New Haven Division, a neighboring office. In fact, several squad mates had volunteered to help. Perhaps if he knew them better, Conrad would have accepted. He politely declined, thankful to have the day to help his friend.

He inspected his map one more time, when his pager went off. The code read, "777." It was Sullivan's signal. The subjects were on their way. In his lap, Conrad had a DMV photo of Gerald McCormick.

As if on cue, three men in suits walked out of the New Haven FBI office. Through his binoculars, he confirmed that one was Gerald. The three men conferred briefly in the parking lot. He observed Gerald shake the hands of an older man and then embrace the other. He presumed that the latter was Gerald's father. He could see a resemblance.

The older men walked to a separate car, a black Lincoln Continental with tinted windows. Conrad wondered if it was a company car. It looked like a vehicle that might be used in a funeral procession. Gerald walked to a different vehicle, a brown Honda Accord. He watched as the Lincoln pulled away. He wasn't interested in them.

Once the Honda pulled out, Conrad waited a second and started following. He knew from his limited surveillance training that a single car was not ideal for such a mission. Ideally, a team would utilize at least five or six vehicles for a proper surveillance. Still, he would do the best he could. As it turned out, Gerald McCormick was so distracted by the events of that morning that he was oblivious to his surroundings.

He needed to vent, and his friends were waiting. Conrad followed as Gerald made his way to Route 91, and he headed north, and fast. He kept his distance while still keeping an eye on the speeding car. Eventually, he spotted the Honda exit in Meriden, Connecticut, about twenty miles north of New Haven.

Sullivan kept following at a discreet distance, as the Honda pulled into the Sacred Heart Cemetery. *Familiar territory*, Conrad thought. Conrad let Gerald pull further ahead, since there appeared to be only one entrance and exit to the grounds. He waited a minute and then proceeded into the cemetery grounds. Underneath a large tree, he spotted the Honda parked next to two other cars. Gerald was talking to two other men.

Jackpot, Conrad thought, as he found higher ground for observation. The spot he chose was shaded and secluded.

For the next several minutes, Conrad snapped multiple photos of Gerald McCormick and his two associates. They appeared quite animated. He couldn't wait to develop the film and share with his friend. His only regret was not being able to lip-read.

*****

Milton and Scott had waited patiently for over an hour. They had started to wonder if Gerald would ever show up, when their friend finally arrived. During their one-hour alone, they had chuckled at the thought of Alicia and Paula receiving a baby's finger. They couldn't understand why Gerald had seemed uninterested in their little project. He had changed, that they had decided.

Gerald walked over to them, and Milton spoke first.

"How did it go?"

"Well, I'm guessing that since my handwriting is nothing like yours, I passed their fucking test."

"Was it the same FBI agent?" Milton asked.

"Yeah, the one you said was at the hospital. Carlos Sullivan."

"So Heather's back?" Scott jumped in.

"Yeah, and Sullivan was talking to her."

"This guy gives me a bad feeling," Scott said.

"Agreed. And the detective was there too. He's an experienced investigator, that's got me worried," Gerald answered.

"I took care of that bitch Heather for you." Scott smiled.

"I know." Gerald put a hand on his shoulder.

"Scott and I have a plan, to throw them off your case," Milton chimed in.

Gerald's heart skipped a beat. He was worried that his friends were going off the rails. *This wasn't high school anymore,* he thought. The stakes were much higher.

"If you go after these cops, it will only make things worse," he finally answered.

"Nah, not the cops," Scott said slyly.

Milton nodded in silent agreement, watching Gerald closely.

"As long as you don't go after the cops, I'm on board."

"Okay, Gerry, best you don't know anyway. You don't have the stomach anymore for the dirty work." Scott grinned.

"I've got to go," he announced.

Before leaving, Gerald gave them each a quick hug. *Best to keep them close*, he decided. After he left, Scott and Milton remained to discuss their plans. None of them ever noticed Conrad, dutifully recording their meeting from a distance.

TWENTY-FOUR

Brainstorming

Sullivan listened for a knock at his door with a sense of excitement. Conrad had told him about his success, and it was just a matter of getting the film developed. Conrad had assured him that he found a pharmacy with two-hour film development. He would be right over. Next to Sullivan on his couch was Detective Saucier. Although their relationship had started on a rocky path, it seemed as though they were becoming fast friends. The detective had several other cases, and he was grateful to have such an enthusiastic investigator helping him on this case. While it wasn't his most important investigation, it was definitely a delicate one.

When Conrad finally arrived, Sullivan was beyond grateful. Saucier had been waiting for over an hour, and they were running out of small talk.

"Conrad, meet Detective Saucier."

They shook hands, and Conrad pulled a chair from Sullivan's kitchenette over to the couch. With a prideful grin, he pulled out the photos from his jacket.

"Here they are."

Sullivan and Saucier started reviewing them one by one. After they were finished, Saucier grabbed one of the photos and pointed to one of McCormick's buddies.

"That's the orderly from the hospital," he announced.

"Are you sure?" Sullivan said excitedly.

"Positive. I suspected someone from the hospital might be involved."

"He kind of does look familiar," Sullivan said.

"That explains why your exemplars don't match," Conrad interrupted. "It's probably his writing."

"Or the third guy," Saucier said.

"We need to find out who that is," Conrad stated.

"That has to be our priority." Sullivan looked at them both.

Just then, they heard another knock on the door.

"Are you expecting company?" Conrad asked.

"Actually, yes, I am," he answered, bounding for the entrance.

Sullivan swung the door open.

"Trish, I'm glad you came."

"Guys, this is Trish O'Keefe, the best intern in the FBI."

"I've heard about you, Trish." Conrad beamed.

"And I've heard about you," she answered.

They all exchanged handshakes.

"It was nice meeting you, Ms. O'Keefe. I'm afraid I've got to go, however," Saucier said.

"You can call me Trish."

"All right, Trish, I'm sure we'll meet again soon."

"I hope so." She smiled.

After Saucier left, Trish and Conrad spoke for two hours nonstop. They had many mutual interests and connections back in Boston. At one point, Sullivan got bored and turned on the television. After a time, Sullivan rejoined the conversation.

"So, Sully, what's your next move?"

"I'm going to find out who this third guy is."

"How are you going to do that?" Trish asked.

"I think I know where he might work."

"Interesting…cool."

"Thanks for coming over, Trish. I knew you would hit it off with my brother here."

"I'm all in, Sully. I think this is exciting."

"Yeah, I just hope these guys don't strike again."

His words hung in the air. None of them spoke again for some time.

*****

A cool September breeze had supplanted the muggy days of August. The night air was fresh and crisp. The leaves had started turning yellow, in anticipation of what would be an unusually cool fall season. There was nothing in her surroundings that gave Nina Robinson any concern. She had lived in the town of Wallingford her entire fifty-three years. It was a bedroom community, and nothing of note ever happened in town. So she had not a care in the world as she stepped outside to put some bags in the trash bin.

As she placed the bag in its bin, she heard a footstep behind her. She turned and was stunned to see a figure in black, standing in front of her.

"Who are you?"

"I'm the devil's henchman," Milton whispered.

"What do you want?" Nina Robinson asked, pleading. She saw a glint of light, reflecting from the blade of the knife the stranger held in his hand.

"I want you, Mrs. Robinson."

"I'll scream," she begged.

"It won't help."

He stepped toward her. Her instinct was to run. She turned on her heels to do so but was shocked to find another man. Scott grabbed her by the shoulders. As she struggled with him, Milton came from behind her and put her in a headlock, choking her. Once she stopped resisting, he pulled her hair back, exposing her neck. He drew his knife across her neck and sliced her open. The blood started gushing across her chest and down to her feet.

As she fell to the floor, gasping helplessly, Milton and Scott watched her draw her last breath, her eyes wide in panic and disbelief.

They smiled at the sight.

TWENTY-FIVE

Cycle Center

Sullivan heard the thunderous roar of a flock of birds. He turned to see them lift off in near unison from a clump of tall trees. In a few short minutes, the sky had soured from a bright blue to a ghostly gray. The birds seemed to be heeding Mother Nature's warning. Sullivan decided to do the same, taking refuge under an overpass, just as a downpour descended from the sky. The sound of cars driving over the bridge's metal linchpins reverberated in his ears. He could hear it even over the sound of the falling rain. The thunk-thunk-thunk of cars passing on the highway above was continuous. It was rush hour.

From underneath his improvised shelter, almost five hundred feet in the distance, Sullivan had a clear view of the Cycle Center. The large bicycle logo hung over the main entrance. As he watched the gym, he thought about the progress he had made. With Saucier's help, he had identified one of McCormick's associates as the hospital orderly. It made sense. As a hospital employee, he had access to the victim's home addresses.

He had also connected all three victims to the cycle center. In his bones, Sullivan knew this had to be significant. Perhaps this would be his lucky day. The day he could fill the missing piece of the puzzle.

So he sat and waited, carefully watching everyone who entered and exited. After a few minutes, the rain finally settled into a quiet drizzle. Just as he had hoped, the mysterious third man appeared from the gym's entrance. He couldn't believe his luck. The young man stepped outside and fumbled for a cigarette, eventually lighting one. He stood in a breezy, nonchalant manner, puffing away. As he watched his prey, Sullivan had a thought. He jumped in his car and drove off. He had seen everything he needed to see. As he pulled away, he could see his mystery man flicking his cigarette into the street. He never realized he had been under Sullivan's intense scrutiny.

TWENTY-SIX

Aftermath

Wallingford Police Chief Walter Smith seldom visited a crime scene. Mostly, this was because there was rarely any crime scene in town. But beyond that, he was an administrator to the core. His job was to make sure his troops had what they needed. This required the skill of a diplomat and negotiator, in particular when dealing with the town on budgetary matters. But when he received the call from his lead detective, his words sounded urgent. He had never heard Detective Saucier frightened, but the crack in his voice was unmistakable. Smith pulled his cruiser over at the address described by Sally, his dispatcher. All she knew was that the call was urgent. He parked his cruiser, which was marked CHIEF on the side door, next to Saucier's unmarked police car. Next to that was another marked Wallingford Police car and an ambulance. Its emergency lights were still flashing.

Smith saw Saucier standing at the edge of a driveway, and he made his way there, with some trepidation. He could see the outline of a body with a white sheet draped over it. Pools of blood were everywhere. Two medics stood near the body, as they checked some equipment and prepared a portable stretcher with wheels. Smith noticed that Saucier seemed just as pale as the sheet covering the deceased.

"What happened?" Smith asked.

"It's Nina Robinson; she's been murdered."

"Oh shit, I knew her. She's lived in town her whole life."

"Yes, as did I. A neighbor found her this morning."

"No family?"

"She divorced several years ago, according to the neighbor. The ex is on his way."

"You know it's always the husband," Smith pronounced.

"Not in this case." Saucier shook his head.

"Why not?"

"The ex is on his way from London. He's been on business. His new wife said his plane arrives this evening."

"Fuck." Smith looked at the sheet covering the body. "How did it happen?"

"Whoever did this"—he hesitated—"practically cut her head off."

"Shit."

"Do you want to see?" Saucier pointed to the body.

"Hell no." Smith recoiled.

"Well, I'll start by interviewing the neighbors. Then the ex."

"Good idea. Did the subject leave any evidence?"

"Funny you should ask."

"So there is something."

"Follow me." Saucier waved him over, walking him to the edge of the crime scene. He pointed at the ground.

"Ah," Smith sighed, "a partial footprint."

"Yes, a sneaker. The perp must have stepped on some of her blood." Saucier nodded.

"How could he not."

"True, this is a very bloody scene."

"You know what this means, right?" Smith stared at his detective.

"What?"

"You drop everything." He pointed at Saucier. "We've haven't had a murder since I've been chief. You will clear this case. Everything else can wait."

TWENTY-SEVEN

Nurse Flaherty

Having been unable to reach Detective Saucier, Sullivan decided to revisit the hospital on his own. The sad, sick smell of hospital emergency rooms was depressing to Sullivan. He would rather have been anywhere else on the planet at that moment. But he had a lead, and he wasn't going to let go. He waited patiently for Nurse Flaherty, who had been tending to a patient. She asked him to wait in an adjoining, private room with a window overlooking the main center. When she walked into where Sullivan was waiting, she gave him a "What do you want now?" look. She was busy and not in the mood.

"All right, Agent Sullivan, what's up?"

"How good are you at keeping a secret?" he asked, cryptically.

"I'd say very good," she said after hesitating for a moment. Sullivan had her attention.

"And how calm are you under stress?"

"You're joking." She smiled, waving her hand around the ER. "I'm an ER nurse."

"Good, I thought so." He stared at her as if evaluating her for a secret mission.

"What is this about?"

"If I tell you this secret, you can't tell anyone. Not your colleagues. Not your family. Not anyone."

"All right, I'll bite. What the hell is going on?"

"I followed up on Heather Knight. I think she was poisoned. As were the other women. Those weren't miscarriages."

"Murder?" she said, her mouth making a horrified face.

"I think so."

"Is it someone who works here? You said maybe it was somebody who works here." Her voice pitch went up a decibel.

"Yes."

"Who?"

"Milton Verdun."

"The orderly? Oh my God, he is creepy!"

"What can I do?"

"For now, I just need to see his employee file."

"It's in administration."

"I didn't want him to see me there. That's why I came to you. I need you to get his file. I need to see it."

"I can do that."

"Then I might need you for something more important."

His words hung in the air for a moment, unanswered, before she turned and walked out with a sense of purpose.

TWENTY-EIGHT

High School

Sullivan pulled his bureau Chevy into a visitor's parking spot at Lyman Hall High School. The school was one of two high schools in Wallingford, established in 1957. It was named for Dr. Lyman Hall, who had been born in town and was an original signatory to the Declaration of Independence. Before getting out of the car, Sullivan took sight of his surroundings. It looked like a typical school, down to the school mascot; a Trojan's banner hung over the entrance.

Having seen the mystery third man from a distance, Sullivan had a thought. McCormick and his two friends appeared to be the same age. Perhaps their friendship extended to high school. Having reviewed Milton Verdun's work application at the hospital, he had narrowed down the school. He had graduated there in 1988, at least according to his application.

Sullivan walked into the school and found the administration offices. He placed his hand on the counter and smiled at the receptionist. She was a middle-aged female, wearing dark office pants and a beige blouse. As she looked up at him, her glasses swayed from a lanyard around her neck.

"May I help you?"

"Yes, I'm Carlos Sullivan, with the FBI," he said warmly, displaying his credentials.

"Oh my, let me get someone."

Without further prodding, she walked quickly to the back offices. It was clear from her reaction that the FBI did not pay regular visits to the school.

In short order, a large middle-aged male emerged from the rear and greeted him with an open hand.

"I'm Reginald Stevens, the vice-principal."

"Carlos Sullivan, FBI."

"Let's go to my office." He waved for Sullivan to follow.

Once seated across from each other, Sullivan leaned in right away.

"I'm investigating a former student of yours. His name is Milton Verdun. Can you tell me if you knew him?"

Steven's eyes widened like saucers. His face turned red. For a moment, he seemed frozen in place.

"Who has he killed?" he finally blurted out.

"I guess he made an impression." Sullivan smiled wryly. "Tell me about him."

"More like them. The three amigos as we called them. Verdun, Wilcox, and McCormick."

"I see."

"No, I don't think you do. Let me get Mrs. Whittaker. She needs to be in on this."

Sullivan got comfortable as Stevens picked up the phone and dialed the receptionist.

"Betty, can you get Mrs. Whittaker to come to my office?"

His tone was serious. It was clear to Sullivan that Stevens ran a tight ship. In what seemed like moments, Mrs. Whittaker appeared before them.

"Mrs. Whittaker, this is FBI Agent Sullivan. He's asking about Mr. Verdun."

"Oh my! Who did he kill?" she asked, taking a seat.

"That's what I asked him," Stevens said flatly.

"Interesting. Why don't you tell me about him?"

"Mr. Sullivan, I consider myself a progressive person. And a Christian—"

"No need to sugarcoat things, Mrs. Whittaker."

"Tell him," Stevens urged.

"He is just not a good person. He and his friends, Scott Wilcox and Gerry McCormick. The three of them were a plague here."

"Go on," Sullivan encouraged her.

"All three were in my English class. They were in some cult. They were found to be killing animals. Wilcox was poisoning small dogs in his neighborhood. Once, they did it on school grounds. Verdun and Wilcox were caught red-handed by a parent of one of my other students."

Whittaker then paused, looking over at her boss.

"Go on," Stevens encouraged her, "tell him the rest."

"The rest?" Sullivan asked.

"Well, yes. One of the animals they tortured was pregnant. They operated on the poor animal."

"Operated?"

"They removed the fetuses. It was horrible." She trembled visibly at the memory.

"Wow!" Sullivan exclaimed.

"The police were called, and they were both expelled. As far as I know, they never finished high school."

"What about McCormick?"

"He was suspected, but the other two never gave him up. He was the leader. Plus, his father had a fancy lawyer, and he skated. He graduated with his class. Last I heard he was in the family business."

"The funeral home, yes," Sullivan added.

"That's right."

"Let me show you something," Sullivan said, reaching into his jacket pocket.

He then handed her one of the surveillance photos. She picked it up by the corner.

"That's them, the devil's henchmen. Verdun, Wilcox, and McCormick." She pointed to each separately. "I see they're still thick as thieves."

"The devil's henchmen?" Sullivan asked, puzzled.

"That's what they called themselves." She nodded in disgust.

"Thank you both. This has been very helpful."

As Sullivan stood up to leave, Mrs. Whittaker gave Sullivan a stern look.

"Agent Sullivan, you'd best be careful with them. They're dangerous."

"I will, ma'am."

Sullivan walked outside and took a deep breath. The pieces were falling into place.

*****

Saucier listened patiently as Sullivan recounted what he had learned. His enthusiasm was contagious, which made telling Sullivan the bad news even more difficult.

"That's great, kid. Now you know that it's a ring of three guys. And you know their identities."

"Right."

"But you can't prove their guilt. Actually, we can't prove anything."

"Don't you see? Wilcox poisoned them. Verdun got their addresses and probably mailed the letters. And McCormick got rid of his girlfriend's baby that he didn't want. Plus, he had access to the babies. And the one that was cremated, he probably cut off its fingers, or he gave his friends access to the corpse."

"Possible, but you can't prove it."

"Not yet, you mean; we're just getting started." Sullivan smiled.

"No, kid, *you're* getting started."

"What does that mean?" Sullivan asked, confused.

"Didn't you hear? There was a murder in town. I'm off the letters case. I've been given strict marching orders."

"I heard about it on the news. But you brought us the case. You can't ditch now," he pleaded.

"I'm sorry."

"What if they killed her to get you off the case?" Sullivan's voice rose.

"Now that's just speculation."

"I'm telling you, these guys are some sort of cult. They call themselves the devil's henchmen. They aren't going to stop."

"Then I hope you're up to the job, Sully."

"What about the state crime lab? Can you hook me up there?"

"What about it? The FBI has a lab, doesn't it?" Saucier was puzzled.

"If I find the poison they used, I want it checked fast. Our lab is too far away and too slow."

"Yeah, I can put you in touch with our lab, no problem. I'll call you in the morning with that."

Sullivan reached over and shook the detective's hands.

"I know your hands are tied. I'm grateful for anything."

TWENTY-NINE

Proof

AUSA Kaplan leaned back in his chair, his feet propped up on his desk, as he listened to Sullivan recite the facts of his case. On his desk was a steaming cup of coffee, which he occasionally retrieved to take a sip. A notepad was also on his desk calendar. It was turned to a blank page. A pen rested next to the pad, but Kaplan hadn't touched it. As Sullivan finished talking, Kaplan took a long swig of his coffee.

"So let me get this straight. You think there's a conspiracy of three involved in this letters matter?"

"It's murder," Sullivan stressed.

"Even if it is, that's not within our purview."

"They have prior bad acts; they were arrested as juveniles." Sullivan handed him the police reports.

Kaplan leaned over and took the reports, scanning them for a minute.

"These devil's henchmen were juveniles—I'm not sure we could even introduce this as evidence," Kaplan said as he handed the papers back.

"I know I don't have enough for an arrest yet."

"So what are you asking for?"

"I'd like a search warrant."

"For what?" Kaplan was incredulous.

"McCormick's business."

"The funeral home?"

"Yes."

"On what basis? And what would you be looking for?"

"I'll know when I find it."

Kaplan was sipping his coffee at that moment and practically spit it out onto the floor.

"Ha! You are funny, kid."

"I'm not laughing."

"That's not how it works. You know that, even as a rookie."

"Actually, I'd be searching for the poison they've been using. That would be an instrumentality of the crime, no?"

"Now you're talking." Kaplan nodded.

"So I can get a warrant?"

"No, but at least you're on the right track."

"A warrant will shake things up. They'll get nervous and make a mistake."

“Well, maybe, but you can’t use the law for a fishing expedition.”

“So what do you recommend?” Sullivan asked.

“You need something called proof. And a creepy cult name is far from proof.”

“In the meantime, they might strike again.”

“Work faster then.” Kaplan took his feet off the desk and stood up. It was his cue the meeting was over.

THIRTY

Crime Lab

The Connecticut State Division of Scientific Services (DSS) was located in building 10 on the Mulcahy complex in Meriden, Connecticut. The building was a dull brown and looked more like a college dorm than a laboratory. The DSS was divided into three components: Chemistry, Biology/DNA, and Identification. The Chemistry section was responsible for, among other things, toxicology. Walter Conley was a veteran examiner, assigned to the Chemistry section. He looked the part of the prototypical scientist, with the only exception that he didn't wear a lab coat. He was slender, mild mannered, and wore slim wire-rimmed glasses, which never left his face. More important to Sullivan was that he was related by marriage to Detective Saucier. Sullivan had started to notice that Connecticut was a small place, and everyone seemed to be connected somehow.

Conley was a cousin of Saucier's wife, and they had become close friends. Saucier had arranged for a meeting between Conley and Sullivan. The city of Meriden was only thirty minutes from the FBI office in New Haven, and he called Conley to advise him when he was on his way. When he pulled into a visitors' parking space, Conley was already outside, waiting for his FBI visitor. Conley had already decided that he would hold the meeting outside. It was a nice day after all, and he could use the fresh air. As Sullivan got of his bureau Chevy, Conley approached.

"Agent Sullivan, I presume," he said, extending a hand.

“Yes, Mr. Conley; thanks for seeing me.”

“Not a problem. Anything for John.”

Conley waved to a nearby bench, and they sat down under a large mahogany tree.

“What can I do for you?”

“I’m working a case where three pregnant women were poisoned. I believe this caused the women to miscarriage.”

“I see.”

“This is a copy of a toxicology report for one of the victims.” Sullivan handed over the report.

Conley scrutinized it for a minute.

“Well, this blood work does indicate an elevated presence of lead. Do you have a sample of the poison so I can analyze it?”

“That’s why I’m here, actually.”

“Aha.”

“You see, I’m going to try and get a sample. Once I do, I need a real quick analysis.”

“I see. Your laboratory is in Quantico.”

“Exactly.”

“I’ll help you any way I can.”

"Outstanding, Doctor."

"I'm an examiner, not a doctor." Conley laughed.

"Well, thank you."

"This is my card. On the back is my pager number. You can reach me anytime with that."

Sullivan pulled out of the lot with a sense of purpose. He had finally made another ally in his battle of wits with the devil's henchmen. He was also making connections, which might help him in future cases. This last thought bothered him, because he realized there would be no future investigations if he didn't solve his first case.

THIRTY-ONE

Wilcox

Scott Wilcox sat on a high chair, behind a long counter at the Cycle Center. His job was to check client passes and verify membership. His other job was to hand out towels and water. He kept a stock of water bottles under the counter. He handed them out as needed. In a separate drawer, Wilcox kept a special water bottle. It was his secret stash for special occasions. He kept the drawer locked, lest someone make the mistake of taking the bottle. It wasn't meant for just anyone.

He was reading a news article about the recent murder of Nina Robinson, when he noticed someone he had never seen before. His heart rate spiked at the sight. It was a young female, and she appeared to be at least six months pregnant. He was practically salivating when she handed him her Cycle Center pass.

"I haven't seen you here before," he said, drooling.

"I just moved here. I signed up yesterday."

"Just my luck; it was my day off."

"My name is Cindy."

"I'm Scott. I'm here for whatever you need."

"That's nice," she said, holding her belly.

“I’m guessing about six months, right?” He smiled.

“That’s right!”

“Is your husband also a member?” he inquired.

“No, I’m not married.”

“I see,” he said.

“I’m here for the yoga classes. I want to stay flexible.” She smiled broadly.

“Well, you came to the right place.” He handed her a towel.

As she turned to walk by, he called out to her again.

“Cindy, don’t forget your water,” he said, stretching out his hand.

“Thanks!” She grabbed it and put it in her gym bag.

Wilcox had handed her a regular water bottle. Although he was tempted to reach into his locked drawer, it was too soon. *Yet the day would come*, he thought. She had taken him by surprise. It just had to be the right moment.

*****

Later that evening, Wilcox met Verdun at a coffee shop near the Wallingford Police Department. There was a full moon over a cloudless sky. Wilcox’s blood pumped faster as he told Verdun about his new gym member.

"So when are you thinking of doing this?" Verdun asked.

"Soon, very soon."

"Make sure I'm on shift. I want to be there to see it."

"Of course." Wilcox smiled.

"What's her name?"

"Cindy."

"That's awesome." He high-fived his partner.

"What about Mrs. Robinson?"

"What about her?"

"Have you heard anything?"

"Nothing. They have no clue."

"As it should be." Wilcox nodded his head.

THIRTY-TWO

Friends

Dagny's Tavern was a quiet watering hole near downtown Hartford, Connecticut. The decor was old, and the air smelled slightly stale. But it was the most central and thereby convenient location for Conrad, O'Keefe, and Sullivan to meet, and the beer was cheap. Trish O'Keefe was not quite old enough to drink alcohol, so she sipped on a Diet Coke as Sullivan and Conrad shared a pitcher of Sam Adams. The bar's television was fixed on a sports station, and a few patrons were watching a Bruins–Flyers game. The Bruins were winning one to nothing in the third period. Occasionally, the regulars would hoot and holler at a particular play.

Sullivan and his friends were oblivious to the game as they discussed business.

"So Kaplan shot you down," Conrad stated.

"You know he's right, Sully, don't you?" O'Keefe reprimanded.

"Yes, Trish, I know."

"So what's next? Did you show the other victims the pictures of Wilcox and Verdun? Maybe they knew them somehow," O'Keefe said.

"Good thinking, Trish, but I'm way ahead of you. Neither Paula White nor Alicia Webster recognized these guys. It was a dead end."

"I see. So now what?"

"Well, McCormick has a lawyer, but I don't think Verdun and Wilcox do."

"So what are you thinking?" Conrad asked.

"I'm thinking of just bringing them in for questioning."

"I thought you didn't want them to know you're on to them."

"Initially you're right. I thought I might spook them. Now I think the opposite. I think they can't stop themselves." Sullivan stroked his chin, thinking.

"It might push them to do it again." O'Keefe nodded.

"Exactly."

"You'll have a lot to answer for if someone else is hurt," Conrad warned.

"We have to provoke them," Sullivan said. "It's the only way."

"Very dangerous, Sully," Conrad repeated.

"We'll have to stay one step ahead."

Trish smiled and then took another sip of Coke.

*****

The next day, Sullivan was at his desk, when Boreman approached him. He didn't even have to look up to know that it was Boreman. He had learned the sound of his steps. He always wore a pair of shoes that had a distinctive click to them as they pressed against the floor.

"So I heard you applied for a search warrant and were shot down."

"Nope."

"That's what I heard." Boreman smiled.

"No. I had a meeting with the AUSA. I didn't apply for anything."

"Either way, sounds like you have no case."

"We'll see." Sullivan looked through some papers on his desk, ignoring Boreman.

"You're an epic fail so far."

"Perhaps."

Sullivan continued to avoid eye contact with Boreman, which he knew infuriated his nemesis.

"You are going down in flames."

Ignored again, Boreman turned and walked away.

*****

That afternoon, Sullivan paid a visit to squad C-9, known as the "tech squad." Each FBI office has designated "technically trained agents," also known as "TTAs." They are special agents who can assist in picking locks, doors, or safes. They are also are equipped with secret recording devices. Some are hidden within briefcases, or some can be secreted on a person's body.

George Finnegan was one of the more experienced tech agents in the New Haven Field Office. He looked Sullivan up and down when he showed up on the squad.

"So you're the new kid," he said, shaking Sullivan's hand.

"That's me."

"So you said on the phone you need a recorder."

"Yeah, do you have something I can borrow?"

"It's called a NAGRA," Finnegan explained. "It's the smallest I have right now." He showed Sullivan a small rectangular silver case, about the size of a cigarette pack. He slid a latch on one side to reveal the interior, a reel-to-reel recorder, demonstrating how to spool it.

"So this is the on/off switch?" Sullivan asked, inspecting the device and pointing to a small button.

"Yep. I like to say it's agent proof." He smiled.

"Cool."

"It does have one problem." Finnegan frowned.

"Oh?"

"Yeah, it can get hot after a bit. So if you tape it against your skin, it could be a problem."

"Hmm. Good to know."

"Just don't lose it. I need it back."

"I'll guard it with my life."

"Anything else?" Finnegan asked, helpfully.

"What about listening in real time?"

"That would be a transmitter."

Finnegan opened a drawer and pulled out a small black device. It had a red button on top and a small rigid antenna on one end.

"It's simple to use. You just flip this switch, and the light comes on. It means you're transmitting. You can use one of our radios to listen." Finnegan flipped the back of the device and showed him a sticker affixed to it.

"Just tune your radio to this frequency listed on the back."

"What's the range?"

"That depends. In an open field, I'd say around one thousand feet. In a building, it could be maybe around one hundred, depending on the type of structure."

“That’s very helpful, thanks.” Sullivan smiled, pocketing the devices.

“One thing kid,” Finnegan said, taking a step back.

“What’s that?”

“Don’t tell Boreman I gave you any of this.”

THIRTY-THREE

Confrontation

Having been told by Nurse Flaherty what his schedule was, Sullivan appeared at the hospital the next day, looking for Milton Verdun. Sullivan waited in an administrative conference room, while the staff summoned him for an interview. After what seemed like an eternity, Verdun appeared before him. Verdun recognized him immediately.

"You're the FBI agent," he said, taking a seat.

"Yes, I am. Carlos Sullivan." He displayed his credentials.

"What can I do for you?"

"Well, I have a few questions."

"What kind of questions?"

"I'd like to know if you know Paula White, or Alicia Webster."

Verdun winced noticeably. He shook his head.

"I know who they are. They were patients here."

"I know that. I'm just wondering why you poisoned them." Sullivan stared at Verdun, hard.

"You can't prove that."

"Interesting. So you don't deny it."

"I didn't hurt anyone."

"So you admit sending the letters then."

"I do not." Verdun was getting agitated, his face reddening.

"So you won't mind giving me handwriting samples."

"I'm done here." Verdun stood up, reached into his pocket, and pulled out a business card.

"Leaving so soon?" Sullivan mocked.

"This is my lawyer, if you have any more questions."

He handed the card over and stormed out.

Sullivan watched him leave, certain that he was correct in his analysis. *Why would a hospital orderly have a lawyer's card in his pocket?* he thought. Then he looked at the name on the card, and his suspicions were cemented. The name "Jeremiah Benson, Esq." practically shouted at him, and he smirked. It was McCormick's lawyer.

******

Scott Wilcox's response to Cindy Larson was Pavlovian. He saw her and started salivating. Her belly protruded from a tight shirt as she started to walk out of the Cycle Center. He saw her approaching and jumped out of his chair to get the door for her. In one seamless motion, he grabbed a water bottle and rushed in front of her before she could leave.

"Don't forget your water," he said, handing her a small bottle.

"Thank you; you're so sweet," she gushed.

He held the door open and watched her as she walked out. He stepped out to see what kind of car she had, when he noticed a man standing next to the entrance, leaning against the railing, his arms crossed.

"Can I help you?" Wilcox asked.

"My name is Carlos Sullivan. I'm with the FBI."

"I've heard of you."

"I'm sure you have. I had a chat with your friend Milton. He had a few things to say about you."

"I doubt that."

"Yeah, he did," Sullivan lied.

"What do you want?" Wilcox asked, annoyed.

"I want to know why you're poisoning women."

"I've got nothing to say."

"That's okay; I just wanted you to know I'm watching you." Sullivan stared at him.

"If you have any questions, I have a lawyer."

"Let me guess, Jeremiah Benson."

Wilcox looked surprised but said nothing. He walked back into the Cycle Center. Sullivan didn't upset him as much as the fact that he was unable to see what Cindy was driving. She was looking ripe. Perhaps it was time to dip into his special drawer. Sullivan would never stop him.

THIRTY-FOUR

Reunion

As teenagers, Milton Verdun and Scott Wilcox spent a lot of time in the basement of McCormick's funeral home. The three friends would often poke at the corpses kept there. Their desire to mutilate the corpses was tempered only by Gerald's fear that his father would discover their antics while preparing the bodies for display. Each of his clients went through a meticulous preparation process, where no detail was overlooked, to include makeup. Gerald was often present during this process, often noticing how the deceased were in many cases more attractive than when they were alive.

Milton and Scott would plead with Gerald to let them cut one of the bodies. He never relented. He would have liked to, but he knew the consequences would be dire. Gerald was smart enough to know that he would one day inherit the business, as his father had promised him more than once.

Gerald did allow, however, the funeral home's basement to be used for the mutilation of animals. They would bring them in the rear entrance under the cover of darkness. They would sit in a circle and remove the organs of the animals they would find in the neighborhood. If they had only done this in the basement, privately, perhaps they would never have been discovered. Wilcox and Verdun, however, became obsessed with their dark hobby. They were caught near the school running track one evening, and the police were called. This resulted in Gerald distancing himself somewhat from his friends. He was the smartest of the three. He knew they were dangerous, so he thought it best to keep them in his orbit, such that he could use them if necessary.

This had worked out when he needed them to take care of Heather Knight. For this he was grateful. The group decided they needed to talk about the status of the investigation, so they decided on meeting at the basement, for old time's sake.

They sat in a circle, just as they once did on a regular basis. Gerald opened the meeting.

"Please tell me you guys didn't whack that lady the other day."

Verdun and Wilcox chuckled.

"I guess that answers my question. What were you thinking?"

"It worked, dummy. It took Detective Saucier off the case. The FBI agent is too inexperienced and clueless," Wilcox answered as Verdun nodded in agreement.

"He came to me at the hospital and visited Scott at the gym," Verdun added.

"I gave him your lawyer's card. Remember you said he would take care of us if we ever needed a lawyer."

Gerald rolled his eyes.

"Don't you see, that only tells him that we're a team!"

"Who cares? He has no fucking idea what he's doing," Wilcox stated.

"You promised you'd take care of us for Heather. When can we expect payment?" Verdun asked.

"Very soon, I promise."

"Aha," Verdun said skeptically.

"More importantly, stop killing people, you jackasses."

Milton started giggling uncontrollably. He and Scott high-fived each other.

"I'm serious," Gerald scolded.

"I noticed how you changed the subject." Milton stopped laughing.

"I said I'd take care of you guys. I will. Just chill out."

They spent the next twenty minutes talking about which Halloween party they would attend in a few weeks. They had no remorse over their victims. Milton and Scott never mentioned their new intended target, Cindy. They knew Gerald wouldn't approve.

THIRTY-FIVE

Anguish

A month had passed since her miscarriage, and Alicia Webster was inconsolable. At first, she thought it was somehow her fault that she lost the child. Perhaps it was the cycling class. Then she learned she might have been poisoned, and her grief turned to a silent rage. *Who could want to harm me?* she wondered. Agent Sullivan had promised to find the person responsible, but she had heard nothing in two weeks. She had stopped eating. She wore the same shirt every day. She would lie in bed for hours after waking, staring at the ceiling.

So Max Webster wasn't immediately alarmed when he came home and she wasn't in the living room, as was typical before the incident. She used to like to read by the window. He called out but heard nothing. He placed his briefcase by the staircase and went to the kitchen. He found a glass in the cupboard and poured himself a glass of water.

He called out again. Nothing. He placed the glass on the kitchen counter and walked to the staircase. One step at a time, he reached the second floor. Each step increased his trepidation. He peered in the bedroom. The bed was unmade, again. This too was a new phenomenon. Alicia used to be a neat freak.

He went to the bathroom and found the door half open. He pushed it open and let out a gasp. Alicia was in the tub, full of water and blood. Both wrists had been sliced open. A knife lay next to the tub on the floor. He pulled her out, showering the floor with water. He cradled her head and her lifeless body, sobbing.

*****

By the time Sullivan arrived at the Webster residence, the medical examiner had already taken Alicia's body away. Max Webster sat on the front steps of his house, his eyes red, in anguish. Next to him was Detective Saucier, a hand on his shoulder. Two neighbors had also made their way to the residence, and they chatted quietly on the front lawn, not knowing exactly what to do. There was no protocol for this situation.

Sullivan had received an urgent page to call the police station. Once he did, the message was to report to the Webster residence. No other information was provided. He knew that Saucier would not have summoned him for a triviality.

Saucier walked toward him when he arrived.

"What happened?"

"Alicia committed suicide," he said flatly.

"Fuck!" Sullivan yelled.

The neighbors looked over, surprised. Max did not move.

"Listen, kid, this isn't on you."

"I promised her I would find these assholes." His face reddened.

"And you will."

"Not in time."

"You will." He placed a hand on Sullivan's shoulder.

"Oh yeah, I will; you bet I will."

"You can't do anything crazy. You're a bit of a hothead."

"These guys will pay." Sullivan clenched his fists.

"Kid, you can't take a case personally."

"It is personal."

"Maybe this job isn't for you, Carlos."

"Maybe not."

"Are you making progress?"

"Some. Can you help me now?"

"Sorry, kid, I'm off the case. My boss gave me strict orders."

"Doesn't this change things?"

"It's a suicide, no." Saucier shook his head.

"All right, thanks, John." He bowed his head in disappointment.

Sullivan walked to his car. He gunned the engine and peeled away, as the combined fury and sadness washed over him.

*****

That evening, before going home, Sullivan stopped at the New Haven Medical Center. He found Nurse Flaherty and briefed her on what had occurred. She had already promised to help him any way she could. On his way out of the hospital, he spotted Milton Verdun, who was making his rounds. Milton gave him the finger and smiled.

THIRTY-SIX

Victim

More than half the leaves had fallen from the trees that lined the parking lot at the Cycle Center. This signaled that the fall season was in full swing. What leaves remained were a bright orange, red, or purple. Those on the ground created a colorful carpet for the cars that were parked there. This included Cindy Larson's car, which she pulled into a corner spot. Unbeknown to her, Scott Wilcox was watching her from a window as she labored across the lot and up the steps. She had to use the railing to get up to the top. This only excited Scott more as he watched her struggle. He had already prepared a special odorless cocktail for her. It was in his drawer, and this was the chosen day.

Wilcox opened the door for Cindy as she reached the entrance.

"Hi there, Cindy!" He smiled.

"Hi, Scott, thanks for getting the door." She put a hand on her full belly.

"Not a problem."

"You're sweet," she gushed.

"Remember to stop by on your way out."

"I will."

As she went into the changing room, Wilcox again looked out the window. He watched as Sullivan pulled into the parking lot and got out of his car. Sullivan stepped out and leaned against his bureau Chevy, arms crossed, staring at the Cycle Center. Wilcox walked outside and down the steps, toward Sullivan.

He pointed at Sullivan as he approached the Chevy.

"You're trespassing, Agent Sullivan," he yelled.

"Why don't you call the cops?"

"I just might."

"Go right ahead."

Sullivan leaned further back, lacing his hands behind his head, mocking Scott, who turned and walked back to the gym. He had no intention of calling the police, for he knew that his complaint would be unanswered.

An hour later, Cindy walked out of the changing room, having showered. Her hair was still wet, which excited Scott all the more when he saw her coming his way. He reached into his drawer and retrieved his special water.

"Here you go, Cindy," he said, handing her the water bottle.

"Thanks again, Scott."

He held the door open for her as she exited. He glanced at the lot and saw that Sullivan was still leaning against his car, staring at him. He thought of making an obscene gesture but decided not to agitate Sullivan. It would only ruin his moment with Cindy.

Sullivan watched as Cindy walked across the lot, holding her belly with one hand, a gym bag slung over her shoulder. He arched an eye at the sight. He said nothing, however, as she got in her car and drove off.

Cindy had placed the water bottle in her cup holder, and it rocked back and forth a bit as she turned a corner.

THIRTY-SEVEN

Emergency Room

Having been advised by Scott that Cindy had received her special potion, Milton started visiting the emergency room with more frequency. He could barely contain himself. He had already checked, and room 505 was available. He couldn't believe his luck. The thought of wheeling Cindy Larson into the same room as the other women aroused him. He would have total control over her, even if for only a few minutes. He crossed his fingers that she had already ingested Scott's concoction.

Finally, close to the end of his shift, he heard the scuttlebutt. A radio call had been received from one of the ambulances. A pregnant female was on her way with severe abdominal pain. *It had to be her*, he thought. He waited near the emergency-room door, watching for his next victim. Ten minutes after the call was received, the ambulance arrived, and a young female was wheeled into the ER. She matched the description Scott had given him. He soaked in every detail, as Nurse Flaherty and another attendant took her into an examination room. They were followed shortly by Dr. Wilson, his stethoscope draped around his neck.

Several minutes later, the doctor left the examination room, and Nurse Flaherty also walked out right behind him, reaching for a wall phone. She dialed a number she read from a business card as she squinted through her reading glasses. The curtain had been drawn, so Milton couldn't see what was transpiring in the room with Cindy. He would have given all his possessions for even a minute inside the room. *What could be taking so long?* he wondered. Milton did his best to mill about in a manner that made him look busy. For the next fifteen minutes, he emptied trash cans and swept the floor as slowly as possible.

Milton then heard the emergency-room doors open, and Sullivan walked in, his eyes swollen with anger. He turned his back to Sullivan, hoping not to be noticed. Sullivan did notice, however, as he walked toward the nurse. His first impulse was to reach over and choke the life out of him. He resisted the urge, however, as Nurse Flaherty put a hand on his shoulder. Milton was close enough to hear them talk.

"You asked me to call if we had another case like the others," she started.

"What happened?"

"We have a young female, Cindy Larson. She's presented with the same symptoms as the others."

"Please tell me she didn't—"

"I'm afraid so," she interrupted. "She's lost the baby."

"Fuck!" Sullivan cried out.

"She's been sedated."

"When can I talk to her?"

"She'll be conscious in the morning."

Milton trembled with excitement as he listened to the conversation. He walked away, waiting for orders to take Cindy to her room.

"I'll keep you posted," Flaherty said.

"I'll want blood work, you understand," he stressed.

"Yes, of course. Wait here while I finish attending to Ms. Larson."

Sullivan took a seat as Flaherty walked over to Milton, who was doing his best to appear uninterested. He could see her pointing to the examination room, and then Milton walked into the room. Sullivan was able to catch a glimpse into the room when Milton pulled back the curtain. Cindy was attached to an IV solution. Milton pulled her bed into the hallway and down the corridor.

He pushed the elevator button, and the door opened. Milton pushed Cindy's bed into the elevator, his excitement rising as the door finally closed and they were alone. He pushed the button for the fifth floor.

He then reached over and caressed her hair.

"Oh, my sweet Cindy. Your baby is with Satan now. You were carrying his spawn."

The elevator made a sound as it passed each floor, finally arriving on the fifth level, the doors opening again.

He wheeled Cindy into room 505 and closed the door. He knew he only had a few moments with her. He rubbed her head gently and then reached down and smelled her closely.

"Cindy, your fetus is pure evil. We had to kill your little baby. We had no choice," he whispered.

As he leaned into her again, he saw what seemed like movement. Then her eyes opened. Milton took a step back. Cindy stared right at him. Milton was confused, as she had been sedated. *What's happening?* he thought.

"Did you get that, Sully?" Cindy said aloud, sitting upright.

In that moment, the door swung open, and Sullivan entered. He had a gun in one hand and a radio in another.

"Yes, I did," Sullivan announced.

"Good," she said. "Can we arrest this piece of shit now?"

"What's going on here?" Milton asked.

"Mr. Verdun, you're under arrest."

"What?"

"Mr. Verdun, meet Cindy Larson, a.k.a. Trish O'Keefe, the best the FBI has to offer." Sullivan smiled.

Nurse Flaherty then walked in, holding what looked like a rubber ball. She put it up for Milton to see.

"I gave Agent Sullivan this rubber prosthetic," Flaherty said.

"And we thank you, Nurse Flaherty." Trish grinned as she pulled the tape off her side, where she had attached the NAGRA and transmitter to her body.

"The NAGRA, was it hot?" Sullivan asked.

"Sure was; I was about to get burned."

"Good, that means it was working. We got everything on tape."

THIRTY-EIGHT

Round Two

The bright, quarter moon hung low over the horizon on Elm Street in Wallingford, Connecticut. What few leaves remained on the trees swayed with the branches in the cold evening air. The streetlamps also illuminated part of the sidewalk in front of Scott Wilcox's house. More importantly, it shone a light on the cruiser containing Saucier and Sullivan as they waited outside for a backup cruiser to join them. They each sipped a steaming hot coffee as Sullivan recounted the events of that evening.

"So you used the intern as an undercover operative?" Saucier asked, concerned.

"Yes."

"Does the FBI allow that?"

"I think not. But I thought it was the only way to catch them. I'll worry about that after."

"What about you, helping me tonight?" Sullivan arched an eye.

"Are you kidding me? I can tell the chief this case is wrapped up. He'll be thrilled."

"I'm glad it works for you."

“That was clever, figuring out who was poisoning them,” Saucier said, looking into his rearview mirror.

“The Cycle Center was the one thing all the victims had in common.”

He took another sip of coffee and then looked over at Sullivan, concerned.

“You do know that you will have some explaining to do.”

“I know. This might be my last case.”

“Well, at least you kept your word.”

“Your cousin Walter was the key. He helped us check all the water Wilcox gave Trish. The last batch was pure, odorless poison.”

“Jackpot!” Saucier exclaimed.

“Absolutely. Unfortunately, it came too late for Alicia.” Sullivan shook his head.

“Still, it means something.”

“Not if we don’t get McCormick.”

“What’s your plan?” Saucier asked.

“Do you know of a good prosecutor? We need these two fools to flip on Gerald.”

“I have a great one. I’ll bring him in tomorrow morning.”

"We need to keep them separated and no calls allowed. Can you arrange that?" Sullivan asked.

"Yeah, I can arrange that."

At that moment, they could see the light from an approaching cruiser pull in behind them. The cruiser turned off its lights, and two patrolmen emerged, flanking Saucier's car.

"It's time," Sullivan announced.

"This is the fun part, kid."

Saucier and Sullivan walked up the steps to Wilcox's door. They rapped several times until a lady in her fifties answered the door in her pajamas. She seemed mildly annoyed at being disturbed as she stared at them.

"Can I help you?" she asked.

"Is Scott Wilcox your son, ma'am?" Saucier asked.

"Yes, he is."

"This is police business, ma'am," Sullivan stated, pointing to a staircase. "Call him down please."

She yelled for Scott several times as the group waited in the foyer. After a minute, Scott came down the steps, descending with hesitation, as if he were walking on eggshells. He could see the welcoming committee waiting for him, and he made a face.

"What's this about?" he finally asked as he reached the bottom.

"You're under arrest, Mr. Wilcox."

Without waiting for a response, Sullivan grabbed him by the arm and spun him around for handcuffing. When he tried resisting, Sullivan kneed him in the thigh, which caused Wilcox's leg to collapse, dropping him to the floor on his knees. Sullivan placed handcuffs on Wilcox, ensuring they were extra snug.

"That hurts," he cried out.

"We're only just beginning," Sullivan said dryly.

THIRTY-NINE

Interrogation

Alvin Stillwell was a career prosecutor, with over twenty years of experience in the state of Connecticut. Most of his cases involved violent crimes, to include homicide, domestic assaults, and rape. In all his hundreds of cases, however, he had never seen a case like this. He sat in rapt attention as Saucier and Sullivan explained the nature of the crimes committed against their victims. They described the poisonings, the miscarriages, and the suicide. They also shared the juvenile-arrest reports, indicating that these were not impulsive crimes. They had been hatched mentally many years earlier. Most critically, they described their evidence. After they finished, they closed their folder and waited for Stillwell to render a decision.

"Wow," he started.

"That's what we think," Sullivan answered.

"First of all, you have solid evidence. This is a very strong case. You've got the poison, and the toxicology report is solid. You have a compelling recording. I'm going to be seeking murder charges here. What are your concerns?"

"We want McCormick."

"You believe this all started when he asked his cohorts to take care of his girlfriend problem, is that correct?"

"Yes. Her name is Heather Knight."

"And you want to get one of them to flip on him, correct?"

"Yes," Sullivan again answered.

"So one of them will need a deal. You're worried I'll go too soft on them for their testimony on McCormick?"

"That's crossed my mind. I want these guys to go away."

"What about the AUSA? Have you briefed him?"

"Yes, I spoke with AUSA Kaplan early this morning. He's willing to drop the letters case as part of a deal. He said the state charges are quote 'far more compelling,' end quote." Sullivan smiled.

"I agree. That could give us some bargaining points."

"Perhaps," Saucier said skeptically.

"So what more do you need from me?" Stillwell asked.

"I'd like you to be present during our interrogation."

"That's unusual." Stillwell shook his head.

"I know. But we may only get one bite at the apple. I need you there to convince them of how serious these charges are. We need to put the fear of God into the devil's henchmen."

"I agree with the kid," Saucier added.

"All right, sure. I'll play." Stillwell smiled.

******

Sullivan had convinced the team that Milton Verdun was the weaker of the two suspects. Wilcox had been the one to concoct the poison, so he was also more morally culpable. It would be harder to get his cooperation. So a decision was made to focus their efforts on Verdun. After being fingerprinted and photographed, he had been held overnight without any telephone contact. Although unusual, Stillwell agreed that it was not unprecedented. There was still an uncharged coconspirator in the wind. If he made any calls, it could imperil other victims, at least in theory. However, as the clock ticked forward, they would eventually have to present him at a bail hearing and at the least allow him to make a phone call. They were up against the clock.

Verdun was taken from his cell at the Wallingford Police Department and escorted to an interrogation room. He was placed on a metal chair, which was intentionally cold and uncomfortable. Already seated at the table when Verdun was escorted in were Sullivan and Stillwell. The room was small, so Saucier decided to watch from an adjoining room. He observed through the mirror installed in the interrogation room.

"You can unhandcuff him, please," Sullivan said to the escorting officer.

The officer removed the handcuffs and walked out, closing the door behind him. Verdun sat silently. It looked as if he hadn't slept all night. He had deep bags under his eyes. His hair was disheveled. His demeanor was that of a tired man. He looked over at Sullivan.

“All right. You got me,” he said, defeated.

“Yeah, I do.”

“So now what?”

“Now it’s time for you to consider your future.”

“What’s that mean?”

“It means do you want to spend the rest of your life in jail, or do you want to cooperate?” Sullivan crossed his arms.

“Over a few threatening comments and letters? That’s crazy.” He sighed.

“Threatening letters?” Sullivan laughed out loud. “Oh no, my friend. This is far more serious.”

“What are we talking about?”

“We’re talking murder and attempted murder.”

“What? Fuck no, it was just an abortion,” Verdun said, his voice dripping with contempt.

Sullivan lunged forward and grabbed him by the collar.

“It was not an abortion, asshole,” he yelled, shaking Milton like a rag doll. “Those women wanted to have babies, and you killed them. That is murder.”

Stillwell flinched at Sullivan’s display of anger. He put his hand up, warning Sullivan nonverbally.

“Actually he’s right,” Stillwell said.

"Who the fuck are you?" Verdun asked.

"I'm the fucking prosecutor who will be filing murder charges against you."

"For real?" Verdun looked at Stillwell.

"Oh yes, Mr. Verdun. This is very real."

"But I didn't poison anyone."

"It doesn't matter. You are part of the conspiracy. Everyone gets the same charges. That's the law."

"Is there an *unless* in this deal?"

"If you cooperate, we've already talked to the federal prosecutor. They will drop the letters case entirely. That would be federal charges, so it is also serious. That can be taken right off the table," Stillwell offered.

"I won't betray Scott. He's like a brother." Verdun shook his head forcefully.

"We don't care about him. We've got him dead to rights," Sullivan answered.

"Then who?"

"Think about it." Sullivan stared at him, hard.

"You want Gerry, that fuck."

"Yeah, I want Gerry."

“That shit never even paid us.” Verdun’ voice rose in anger.

“He was supposed to pay you?” Stillwell arched an eye.

“Yeah, if we took care of his girlfriend Heather.”

“That’s murder for hire,” Stillwell explained.

“That’s got to be worth more than what you’ve offered then.”

“I can drop the murder charges, and you’ll just face attempted murder. That knocks off twenty years.”

Sullivan listened with concern. He wanted Verdun to face serious time.

“So how much time am I looking at?” He shrugged.

“Fifteen years. That’s a good deal. With good behavior, you might be out in twelve.”

Verdun did the math in his head. He would be released, and he’d still be only his late thirties. He considered his options. Stillwell seemed like a straight shooter. More importantly, it seemed as though they were clueless about Nina Robinson’s murder. He would walk on that completely.

“All right, deal.”

“We’re going to need more than your testimony, though,” Stillwell added.

“What else?”

“We need you to make a recording with Gerry. We need that to nail this down,” Sullivan explained.

“Sure,” he said, “why the fuck not.”

“I have a question,” Sullivan asked. “The fingers you mailed those women, were they from Alicia Webster’s baby?”

“Yeah, we knew it was being cremated, so I sliced off two of its fingers.”

Stillwell winced at the thought.

In that moment, Sullivan’s pager started beeping. It was the office number. This was followed immediately by another identical page.

“Problem?” Stillwell asked.

“Yeah, problem.”

FORTY

Consequences

When word of the Sullivan arrests made it to the FBI New Haven office, it spread like a California wildfire. As the details emerged, and the FBI intern's involvement was discovered, FBI management went into a meltdown. Special Agent in Charge (SAC) Thomas Sanders had called Sullivan's supervisor, Timothy Dalton, demanding answers. Boreman sat next to Dalton when the call was received at his desk. It was clear that Sanders was not happy with the rumors he had been hearing all morning.

"What the hell is going on with your squad?" Sanders asked, his voice so loud that Dalton had to pull the receiver back from his ear.

"Sir, we have made arrests in the case of the women who were poisoned. This is a positive development. You may recall I briefed you on that case a week ago," Dalton answered calmly.

"You never mentioned an undercover operation."

"Sir, Agent Sullivan is on his way into the office now. I'd like to get a fresh briefing before I say anything that might be in error."

"Well, I need answers."

At that moment, Sullivan arrived at the Dalton's desk.

"Actually, Sullivan just walked in."

"I'm on my way down." Sanders slammed the phone down.

"Sullivan, you are fucked," Boreman started.

"What are you talking about? I made two arrests, and another will be happening shortly." He looked at Dalton, ignoring Boreman.

"Another arrest?" Dalton asked.

"Yes, sir. I've flipped one of these suspects, and he's going to make a recording for us. We're looking at murder for hire. Serious shit."

"Did you use the intern as an undercover?" Boreman drilled him.

"Yes, I did. She fit the profile—"

"The profile?" Boreman interrupted. "You can't do that, you idiot. Who authorized that?"

"I authorized it," Dalton announced.

The room went completely quiet. Boreman looked like he had been hit by a truck. Sullivan swallowed quietly, not sure what was happening. Boreman turned to his boss.

"Boss, how could you?"

"How could you lie to me, Ralph?" Dalton stared holes into Boreman.

"Lie to you, about what?"

"I asked you if you knew the supervisor at Quantico. His name was Nuggle."

Boreman's face tightened. He said nothing.

"You told me you had never heard of him. As it turns out, you were his best man."

"Boss, I can explain—"

"No need; you're off my squad," Dalton interrupted. "I've already cleared it with my boss."

"Sir—"

"You're on an administrative squad, effective right the fuck now." Dalton pointed to the door.

Boreman stood up and walked quietly out of the office, his head bowed. At the same moment, SAC Sanders walked into the office, flanked by his two deputies. He leaned over Dalton's desk as Sullivan took a seat.

"What the hell is going on?" Sanders asked.

"Sir, we have a very dynamic situation occurring. Agent Sullivan has flipped one of the defendants, and a third arrest is imminent. We should consider a joint news conference with the Wallingford Police once this is over."

"A news conference." Sanders's face brightened, and his demeanor changed. "That's a good idea."

"In the meantime, I need Sullivan to leave right now and pursue his lead."

"Right, Sullivan, don't let us keep you." Sanders waved to the door.

"Thank you, sir," Sullivan said as he got up to leave.

"Sully, you *will* come to see me once this is over; we need to talk," Dalton said.

"Of course, sir."

Sullivan knew the pain was not over, just postponed.

FORTY-ONE

Recording

In order to minimize the danger of McCormick becoming violent toward Verdun, a decision was made to hold the meeting in a public place. With that in mind, they selected the local Dunkin' Donuts. It was a place where, according to Verdun, he had met McCormick on multiple occasions. It would not send out any red flags. Under Sullivan's and Saucier's watchful eyes, Verdun placed a recorded telephone call to their target, and he readily agreed to the meeting. Verdun was schooled by Sullivan on the use of the NAGRA recorder as well as the transmitter. He considered the irony, as they were the tools that had led to his demise.

Clearly, Sullivan could not be in the establishment during the meeting. With Dalton's blessing, two of Sullivan's squad mates had agreed to sit inside drinking coffee during the meeting. Sullivan and Saucier watched from a distance as McCormick parked in the lot and went inside. He ordered a coffee and found a table. The all-clear signal was received when one of the agents inside stepped outside and lit a cigarette. Verdun sat in the back seat of Sullivan's bureau vehicle.

"Is that the signal?" he asked.

"Yes."

"I'm ready."

“Do you remember your instructions?”

“Yeah, like you said five hundred times. Get him to discuss his girlfriend and what we did for him.”

“Exactly. Don’t fuck this up.”

“Got it.”

“And what’s the code word?”

“If I need you to rescue me, I say the word ‘Wednesday.’”

“That’s right, because today is Tuesday.”

“Can I go in now?”

“Go,” Sullivan ordered.

They watched as Verdun walked into the Dunkin’ Donuts.

“He’d better get this right,” Saucier said softly.

Sullivan said nothing as he turned up the volume on his radio. He could hear the ambient noise in the shop as Verdun walked in.

“Hey, Gerry,” he started, sounding somewhat nervous.

“What’s up, Milt?” McCormick asked.

“Just that you owe us some money.”

“I’ve told you a dozen times it’s coming. Just relax.”

“We’re done waiting.”

"I can give you five hundred dollars until I have the full amount next month." McCormick looked around impatiently.

"If it wasn't for us, you would be a daddy right now."

"Look, I'm grateful; don't get me wrong."

"But what?" Verdun frowned.

"Well, what did *you* actually do? Send Heather a letter? I never asked you to do that. The person I should be paying is Scott. He's the one who actually poisoned her."

Sullivan and Saucier smiled simultaneously.

"This was a team effort. You promised us ten grand."

"It's all I can do, for now," McCormick stated, standing up to leave.

"All right, don't forget us," Verdun said finally. He knew his job was done.

McCormick walked to the door and out into the fresh morning air. As he stepped outside, Sullivan and Saucier were waiting for him.

"What do you two want?" he asked with contempt.

"Mr. McCormick, you are under arrest."

As they handcuffed him against the glass door of the Dunkin' Donuts, he could see inside the shop, as the two agents inside retrieved the NAGRA recorder and transmitter from Verdun. The realization of what had just happened washed over him. He puked against the side of the business.

FORTY-TWO

Revelation

The drive from the Dunkin' Donuts to the Wallingford Police Department was a short two minutes. Yet in that brief time span, McCormick had several revelations. The first of which was that his supposed friend had turned on him. The second was that they probably had recorded his conversation. Given these facts, he knew that even Jeremiah Benson's skills, which were extensive, would be no salvation this time around. By the time he was placed in the Wallingford Police interrogation chair, he was very compliant. His interrogators could also tell he was feeling cooperative, as his whole demeanor had changed.

Sullivan sat before him, hands on the table. Saucier sat next to him. They stared at McCormick for two minutes without a word spoken. Finally, McCormick had enough.

"Okay, what can I do to help myself?" he pleaded.

"You can start by giving a full, written statement," Saucier answered.

"You probably think I'm a horrible person."

"The thought crossed my mind," Sullivan answered.

"I'm guessing that Milt made a deal with you guys."

"He did." Sullivan smirked.

"I see."

"Not good for you."

"I have a question for you guys." McCormick's eyes sparkled.

"What's that?" Saucier asked, curious.

"Did that deal include the murder of Nina Robinson?"

******

Two hours later, Sullivan and Saucier were at the home of Scott Wilcox, where less than forty-eight hours earlier they had affected his arrest. He had already been presented for his arraignment and was being held on a high bail, which he could not make. Given the severity of the charges, the bail had been set at $500,000, which was more than even his mother's home was worth. They didn't have enough to charge him with the murder of Nina Robinson. But Stillwell had gotten a judge to agree that they had enough for two search warrants.

They knocked at the door. Just as before, it took Mrs. Wilcox several minutes to come to the door. Sullivan and Saucier waited patiently. Once she answered, Saucier spoke first, pushing the door completely open.

"Mrs. Wilcox, we have a search warrant for your home."

"What, on what grounds?"

"It's all in the warrant." He handed her a copy.

“Where is Scott’s room?” Sullivan asked.

They gently pushed her aside and proceeded to search the apartment, with the help of four additional police officers. The first place they looked was the closets. They checked all the shoes. Nothing. After they finished, they met in the kitchen for a conference. Mrs. Wilcox had been asked to sit in the living room while they conducted their search.

The group talked in a circle.

“Oh well,” Sullivan started, “strike one.”

“Maybe we’ll get lucky at Verdun’s,” Saucier answered.

******

Milton Verdun’s mother was not pleased to meet her visitors. She had already blamed them for her son’s legal woes. In fact, throughout Milton’s life, she had always felt that his problems were the result of those around her little Milt. In school, his expulsion was the result of overzealous educators. What harm could there be in playing with animals? Her attitude did not change when her son became an adult.

“What do you want?” she yelled at Sullivan and Saucier.

“We want you to step out of the way,” Sullivan ordered.

Saucier pointed to one of his officers, who escorted her to the living room, where she sat under guard. A copy of the search warrant was placed on her coffee table. She refused to read it, her arms crossed defiantly.

As the officers fanned out across the house, Sullivan and Saucier made a beeline for Verdun's bedroom closet. On the floor, they found an old pair of sneakers, under a dirty sweat shirt. With a gloved hand, Saucier picked it up, turned it over, and smiled. He displayed it to Sullivan, who nodded in appreciation.

"Blood," Sullivan said simply.

******

The New Haven Correctional Center is one of eighteen correctional facilities operated by the Connecticut Department of Corrections. Opened in 1976, it serves to house inmates awaiting sentencing, as well as pretrial offenders. As such, it is a jail and not a prison. In Verdun's case, his cooperation assured that there would be no trial. It was simply a matter of arranging a sentencing hearing on the charges he agreed to plead guilty to. In addition to lesser charges, his cooperation had earned him a segregated cell at the five-acre facility. Deep in the basement, he lay down on his bunk, looking up at the ceiling in despair. *Twelve more years of this*, he thought.

As he rested, he heard the approach of a guard.

"You have a visitor," the guard announced through the cell bars, his voice echoing down the hallway.

Verdun was escorted to a private room. He knew it had to be a special visit, because it was a stand-alone room.

Typically, visits were in a common area, with several tables bolted to the ground. His mother had visited him there twice already.

After a minute, Sullivan walked in and took a seat. He could tell from the look on Sullivan's face that something was up.

"Don't even think of reneging on our deal." He pointed at Sullivan.

"You really are stupid."

"A deal is a deal."

"The deal didn't include the murder of Nina Robinson, genius." Sullivan arched an eye.

"I don't know her."

"Really, because the crime lab just found her blood on your sneaker. The one that was in your closet."

The blood from Verdun's face flushed away, to his gut. He felt as though he had been punched. He said nothing. As he looked down at the floor, Sullivan stood up to leave, leaning over as he did so.

"Your probation officer hasn't even been born yet." Sullivan smiled.

As Sullivan walked out of the room, the sound of his footsteps started to fade down the hallway. When he could no longer hear them, Verdun started to cry.

FORTY-THREE

Closure

The conference room at the district attorney's office was plush, with comfortable leather chairs. The visitors were seated around a large rectangular table, and a pitcher of water was in the center of the table, along with several glasses. The Connecticut state seal was prominently displayed on the far wall. There was a quiet buzz in the air, but the visitors' enthusiasm was muted by the fact that their losses were still fresh. Heather Knight, Max Webster, Paula White, and George Robinson had never met before. Their first exchange of greetings had been awkward. Their situation was unprecedented. They had all been victimized for seemingly no reason. They had heard news of the arrests in their case, and the media was spinning a story about "the devil's henchmen," but they weren't sure what to believe. This was an opportunity to get a briefing directly from the authorities. One by one they were escorted by a young receptionist into the conference room, for a meeting on the case.

They waited only five minutes, before Assistant District Attorney (ADA) Stillwell entered, followed by Sullivan and Saucier. They took a seat across from the victims. Stillwell took command of the meeting.

"Thank you all for coming," he began.

"Thanks for inviting us," Robinson answered for the group.

“As you may have heard on the news, we broke up a team of very evil people. I should say, these investigators did.” He motioned toward Sullivan and Saucier.

They nodded in unison.

“Why?” Robinson asked simply.

“Your ex-wife was murdered to get Detective Saucier off the other case. The poisonings—”

“So she was collateral damage?”

“Yes, I’m afraid so.”

“This all started with me, didn’t it?” Heather asked.

“That is correct.” Stillwell looked over at Sullivan.

“You were poisoned for the simple reason that Gerry McCormick didn’t want you to have his baby. I’m sorry,” Sullivan explained.

“And what about us?” Paula asked, pointing to Max Webster.

“They just thought it was funny. I’m sad to say. They liked what happened to Ms. Knight, so they kept doing it,” Sullivan answered.

“And the letters?” Paula asked.

“I’m afraid they are very sick people. They thought it was hilarious.”

"The good news is that we have very solid evidence in all the cases. I will be asking for life sentences on all three," Stillwell announced.

The group chatted for another several minutes, and they exchanged hugs when the meeting was over. Max made a point of finding Sullivan after it was all over, and they were alone in the hallway. He shook Sullivan's hand and looked him straight in the eye.

"I want you to know that Alicia's death wasn't your fault."

"Thank you for that."

Sullivan had a tear in his eye as he left the building.

FORTY-FOUR

Conclusion

Sullivan went to work with a sense of dread. The dust had settled, and he had been summoned by Dalton for a meeting. This he knew was coming. The ass chewing had been postponed but not canceled. It was only a question of what would be left of his ass. Would he be dismissed, or would he get a reprieve? He was, after all, a probationary agent. This meant that he could be fired for practically any reason.

Sullivan entered Dalton's office and closed the door behind him. He knew to do that without asking. Perhaps because of the situation, Dalton's large frame seemed particularly intimidating. Surprisingly, however, Dalton didn't have the scowl on his face that Sullivan was expecting. He seemed calm.

"Take a seat."

Sullivan sat as requested.

"First of all, congratulations on your case. Well done."

"Can I ask you a question?" Sullivan interrupted, which he noticed annoyed Dalton.

"Go ahead," he answered.

"Why did you say you authorized the undercover operation?"

"Because the cardinal sin for a supervisor is to be incompetent. If I didn't authorize it, then I don't have control over my squad. I'd rather appear reckless." Dalton squinted at Sullivan, his eyes narrowing.

"Interesting." Sullivan nodded.

"Why didn't you tell me about your plan?" Dalton's face turned red. He was clearly still angry.

"I thought you'd say no."

"No, I would not have."

"You would have authorized me to use Trish, the intern?" Sullivan asked, surprised.

"Of course not. I would have found a suitable undercover agent. Someone with experience." He scolded.

"Oh."

"Yeah, oh. You have a lot to learn, kid."

"I know." Sullivan nodded. "Will you get jammed up?"

"I've earned a few get-out-of-jail-free cards over the years. I'll be okay. Plus, we got good media coverage over the arrests."

"I'm glad."

"Let me ask you something, Sullivan."

"Go ahead."

"Do you know what Moses had before he parted the Red Sea?"

Sullivan thought for a moment.

"No, what?"

"He had his Supervisor's permission."

"That's good." Sullivan chuckled.

"I think you could be a great agent. But you need to keep your boss in the loop."

"Understood, sir."

"Now get out of here and get back to work." Dalton waved to the door.

"Yes, sir. I actually have one more arrest to make."

"Okay, go to it," he barked.

*****

Heather Knight's apartment complex was as unattractive as the superintendent who was responsible for the building. It was decaying and decrepit. Sullivan entered the structure with two squad mates, who were now eager to help him, given Boreman's banishment from their unit. They made their way to the management office with quick strides. They were on a mission.

They entered the office, and Todd Armstrong was there, just as described by Sullivan. He was still wearing the same white sleeveless T-shirt, lounging behind his large table. He looked surprised to see three men in suits enter his office, until he recognized Sullivan. Then his demeanor turned to fear.

“Can I help you?”

“Mr. Armstrong, please get up from the chair,” Sullivan ordered.

“What is this about?” he pleaded.

“You are under arrest.”

“For what?”

“Really, dumb ass? Do you remember calling McCormick and telling him about my visit here?”

“He told you that—”

“Yes, as part of his agreement with the government, he had to disclose everything. I mean everything,” Sullivan interrupted him.

“Oh shit.”

“Yes, oh shit. It’s called interfering in an investigation.”

“I’m sorry, man.”

“Yeah, and I’m going to want my twenty bucks back.”

Sullivan watched as his squad mates handcuffed Armstrong and escorted him to their squad car. Having been alerted by Sullivan before they arrived, Heather watched from her window as they squeezed Tony into the vehicle.

Sullivan looked up to her window, and she smiled, flashing thumbs-up.

*****

The crowds at Boston's Copley Square were milling about. It was mid-October, and the sun had already fallen over the horizon, but the city's lights gave the evening a holiday ambiance. Conrad had invited Sullivan and Trish to spend the weekend in Boston, and they readily accepted. They sat on a long wooden bench across from Boston's iconic public library, watching people pass by. If the person seemed interesting, they would guess the person's profession. A young man passed by in a flannel shirt and work boots.

"Construction," Trish said, pointing. "Definitely construction."

"Agreed," Sullivan and Conrad replied in unison.

"That was easy, though. What about that guy?" Sullivan asked, pointing out a man in a long trench coat.

"A teacher," Trish answered.

"Wrong; look at the shoes," Sullivan said.

"Right, those are dress shoes. Plus, he has a briefcase," Conrad answered. "A teacher would have a backpack."

"Your guess then?"

"Businessman," Conrad said.

"Wrong. Those are wing-tip shoes; he's a lawyer. Always look at the shoes," Sullivan concluded.

After playing their game for another hour, there was a pause and then a shift in topics.

"So, Sully, you beat the rap. Now what's next?" Conrad asked.

"Who knows what the future holds?"

"I know what's going to happen," Trish replied.

"What does your crystal ball say, Trish?" Sullivan asked.

"We're all going to work together, right here in the city of Boston."

"Is that so?" Conrad said.

"Yeah, I think this roller coaster just got started."

The End

Michael de la Pena may be reached via email at thecoyotewars@gmail.com or follow him on Facebook at The Coyote Wars.

Made in United States
North Haven, CT
11 February 2023

32439866R00129